"We're surrounded! Fire at will!"

Bhodi, from hiding, watched in amazement as one by one each of the Dark Guardians was picked off. There were so many bursts of sparkling light as they vanished that it looked as if someone were setting off firecrackers.

It took only seconds. Almost as quickly as it had begun, the last of the Dark Guardians had been hit squarely in the chest plate and sent back to Arr. Their howls of fury seemed to echo for almost a minute after they were gone.

That was when Gambler stepped out into the middle of the rocky area. "You can come out now, Bhodi. They're all gone."

Slowly Bhodi came out from behind the rock. "You?" he asked incredulously. "You did all that?"

Gambler grinned. "Of course. Who else?"

"You could have at least told me what you had in mind . . ."

A PHOTON
ADVENTURE
NOVEL #2

PHOTON®

THE ULTIMATE GAME ON PLANET EARTH™

HIGH STAKES

DAVID PETERS

Ⓑ®

BERKLEY BOOKS, NEW YORK

PRINTING HISTORY
Berkley/Pacer edition/April 1987

ISBN: 0-425-09812-5

To Shana and Guinevere
who take turns driving me crazy
and keeping me sane

1

Friendly Game

A Hush fell over the crowd.

It was not a particularly large Hush. It was about five feet long, covered with coarse, matted brown fur. It looked somewhat like a bear rug come to life.

The Hush had climbed up into the rafters of the bar in order to get a better look at the tense card game that was currently commanding the attention of everyone in the room. Unfortunately the Hush had had a few too many drinks, lost its grip on the rafters and fell on top of the thoroughly consumed (and consuming) onlookers.

The several creatures onto whom the Hush had fallen yelled in protest for the bartender. They didn't particularly like having creatures drop onto them from overhead, especially when they were watching a top-flight card game such as this one. The Hush tried to stagger to its feet, but since it didn't have any, this maneuver met with only limited success.

"Sorry," slurred the Hush, but the interrupted crowd was not in a forgiving mood. Rough hands lifted the Hush and within moments it found himself out in the street, its large body flopping about helplessly as it tried to regain its sense of direction.

The Hush had just been given the heave-ho from the Marclark Bar, the most renowned drinking and eating establishment on the planet Cichester. Marclark attracted all sorts of creatures from all walks of life, and many of them chose Marclark's as a place where they could all eat, drink, be merry and try to win some money, hopefully without killing each other.

At this moment, the game that had attracted the gathering was the high-stakes card game at Table 6. Half-finished drinks sat on either side of the table, the ice long since melted into nothingness. The drinks sat on coasters—little wheeled devices that rolled the drink away from the consumers when they were not drinking and scooted the glasses back across the table when the consumers decided that they wanted another sip. It had been some time since either of the beings who had ordered these two particular drinks had taken a sip.

The game was called Groth. It was a fascinating game in that it only required half a deck. Part of the challenge of Groth was that you might need certain cards to fill out a hand and couldn't possibly get them because playing Groth required that you be half a deck shy. As a result, a large part of the game was bluff and bluster, because winning on the strength of cards alone was extremely difficult.

One of the beings playing was a creature named Runya. Runya was the toughest gambler in the whole of Cichester. One table at Marclark's was practically reserved for him even when he wasn't there (which was infrequently). Runya was eight feet tall and built like a star cruiser. He had two heads, and each head had only one fearful eye. He would stare at you with those awesome heads and seem to be able to see right through into the back of your mind. It was disconcerting, particularly if you were trying to bluff against him.

There was a tendency to want to just throw down your cards, apologize profusely for wasting his time, give him all your money and possibly your wife and children, and then retreat hastily while being grateful that you were allowed to escape with your life.

To complement his two heads, Runya had four arms—three on one side, one on the other. No one knew why. His body was massive, cablelike muscle and sinew pulled taut over his wide frame. His skin was light gray and, when he was concentrating on a game as he was now, it glistened with a fine sweat.

Opposite Runya sat his opponent, in what was charitably known as the Suicide Seat.

His opponent's name was Pike, or as he was affectionately known to the young Earth boy standing next to him, Uncle Pike.

Pike was about as physically threatening as an avocado. He had a wide body, huge flipperlike feet, extremely thin arms, and a wide neckless head that simply sat there on his shoulders, as if someone had taken a large scoop of orange sherbet, plopped it on his shoulders and put two eyes and a mouth into it. Perched jauntily on top of his head was a green helmet. A normal hand of Groth required ten cards, and Runya held his in one massive hand. Pike, by the same token, required both of his small hands to hold his ten cards.

The Earth boy standing next to Pike was ten years old. He was a little black kid and looked bizarrely out of place mixed in with the assortment of creatures and aliens standing around him. He wore large, round glasses and a Cleveland Indians baseball cap. He had on an orange jumpsuit, and was leaning nonchalantly on a gleaming silver baseball bat. He looked like an otherworldly on-deck hitter.

Pike had a small mound of coins in front of him, and Runya's was a mountain. The results of a full day's worth of playing for him. Now, in Pike, Runya perceived a final victim. Runya studied Pike closely, looking into his eyes, trying to determine just what Pike held in front of him. Pike's expression didn't vary in the least. It hadn't the entire game, and Runya was beginning to wonder if it indeed could change. He shifted his gaze to the young Earthling who stood next to Pike, but Parcival (for that was the boy's name) was equally inscrutable.

Runya blew out air from between both mouths. His breath caused some of the varnish to crack off the table.

"All right, Pike," muttered Runya, and to the astonishment of everyone standing around him, he shoved the entire mountain of money into the middle of the table. Runya's voice rumbled as he said, "I have places to go today. People to see. Cities to level. In short, I have better things to do than kill the entire day with you. So let's make this short and sweet. Put up or shut up."

Pike stared at the pile of money before him. In that thin, reedy tone of his, he said, "I appreciate your trying to make things easy for me, Runya. But there's no way I can cover that much money. You know that." He leaned forward conspiratorially. "You wouldn't be trying to embarrass me, would you?"

There was low laughter among the crowd. Runya considered a moment and then said, "I'd be willing to take your I.O.U. You know that if you don't make good on it, I'd rip your scrawny arms from their scrawny sockets. Or, if you have something you'd care to wager that's not on the table . . . ?"

Pike paused a moment, considering. Then he leaned forward. "Have you seen my ship? The *Zephyr*? It's quite nice."

From his side, Parcival said, "Pike," with a warning edge in his voice.

Runya laughed deep in his throats. "Who's this, Pike? Your business manager? Can't you make your own decisions?"

"Of course," said Pike hastily. "So what do you say? Will the *Zephyr* match the amount that's in the pot?"

Parcival moaned. "Pike, listen—"

Pike shushed him as Runya grinned wide. "Easily, and more. Why, that ship of yours is worth twice what's in the pot."

"In that case," said Pike quickly, "it seems to me that you're the one who's coming up short."

Runya frowned, annoyed with himself that he had made the admission. "Now, let's not be hasty," he said.

"Pike, you can't put up the *Zephyr*," Parcival was saying. "MOM would kill us if she knew."

"Then she'll never need know," said Pike reasonably. "Besides, it's going to be moot. Unless you can come up with the difference, Runya. Hmmm?"

Runya's frown was enough to make a pregnant dog drop her litter on the spot. "My racing cruiser," he said tersely. "Not as big as *Zephyr* but the fastest thing in the twenty-eight worlds. What do you say, Pike?"

"Done," said Pike.

Parcival closed his eyes. "Oh, man," he moaned, "we're going to wind up walking home."

"Have a little faith, Parcival," said Pike sagely.

"I do," said Parcival. "But only a little."

"Enough talking," roared Runya, and he slapped his cards down so hard that the table shook. The coasters rolled right off the table in their confusion and fell to the floor, their respective drinks crashing to the ground.

"A full Rojansky!" he crowed, and indeed that was exactly what he had. It was the third-rarest hand in the game of Groth.

Pike sat there, momentarily stunned, and Runya took that as his cue to reach for all the money that sat on the table. But before he could, Pike put one thin hand on Runya's massive wrist. "One moment, please," said Pike evenly.

Parcival, who had felt all the blood drain from his cheeks at the sight of the full Rojansky, now began to entertain some hope. Runya, however, did not seem the least pleased.

"Moment?" he rumbled dangerously. "Moment for what?"

One at a time, savoring it, Pike placed his cards face up on the table. The disbelief by everyone who could see grew as each successive card was put down. And when the tenth card was placed, there was an audible gasp and even some smatterings of applause.

Pike had a Royal Kirbee.

It was the toughest hand in all of Groth. It was dealt out only once every second generation on the average and had not been seen in this part of the galaxy since the legendary Split-Fingered Fingee had won with it fifty years earlier and had promptly been blown out of an airlock by irate competitors.

Runya did not take it much better than Fingee's opponents had. He leaped to his feet with a roar, knocking the table and Pike back. Money spilled off with a clattering crash. Pike awkwardly flailed his arms and legs about, and Parcival pulled off his cap and tried to catch as much money in it as he could.

Oblivious to the pandemonium, Runya picked up the fallen table and effortlessly broke it in half. He hurled it across the room towards the front door. Everyone scattered except for the poor Hush, who had just undulated back into the room, looked up to see what the commotion was and got itself knocked out.

"I hate to lose!" howled Runya, and he started destroying all the furniture he could get his hands on. Pike, staggering to his feet, stepped back in horror at the unleashed chaos before him, and Parcival (crouching low nearby) said, "Pike, stop him!"

"Why me?" demanded Pike.

"Because you're the one responsible for starting it," he said.

"That's right, that's right," said Pike sourly. "Blame it on me. Use logic. After everything I've done for you . . ."

"Pike, if you don't stop him, I'm going to tell MOM you put the *Zephyr* into the pot."

"Now, who taught you those sorts of tactics?" was the disapproving question.

Parcival ducked a flying glass. "You did."

Pike sighed and, gulping loudly, stepped towards the infuriated alien. "Runya, this isn't necessary."

"But I hate to lose!" yelled Runya, two of his four hands around the necks of hapless creatures.

"You didn't lose."

Runya stepped back and eyed Pike. "I didn't?"

"Not exactly. It's not that you lost. It's just that you didn't win."

Runya stared at him balefully. "What's the difference?"

"The difference. Yes. Well. You want to know the difference." He turned to Parcival. "Any thoughts on this?"

Parcival shrugged.

"The difference," said Pike smoothly, "is that everyone knows you're unbeatable. Don't you all know that, boys?" From around the room there was ragged agreement. "You're considered unbeatable. And it's widely known that if everyone agrees on something, then it must be true. I couldn't have beaten you."

Runya nodded slowly. "All right. But if you couldn't beat me, then what happened? Tell me that."

"Isn't it obvious? You let me win."

Runya stared at him, his two eyes uncertain. "I did?"

"Absolutely."

Slowly Runya shook his massive heads. "But I don't let anybody win."

"Exactly!" said Pike, as if he had suddenly hit upon the answer to life, the universe and everything. "Maybe you weren't thinking about it consciously, but your unconscious realized that if nobody ever beats you, then eventually no one will ever be willing to play you. And if no one will play you, then you really won't ever be able to win."

Pike spread his arms out. "It's sheer genius on your part. I can only be grateful that I was the lucky recipient."

Now Parcival had been watching all this with dazed incredulity. He knew that Pike was, when he had to be, slicker than Teflon. But this had to be a new high, even for Pike. He shook his head, and then he suddenly felt a soft buzzing from his wrist. He looked down. On his wrist was a portable computer unit, capable of small-scale calculations and also capable of hooking into a much larger computer that Parcival sometimes wore strapped to his back. He immediately knew what the computer was trying to tell him.

Parcival and Pike were Photon Guardians—two members of an elite corps of six who were dedicated to preserving the galaxy from evil forces that most beings were unaware even existed. And their central coordinator, a super-computer called MOM, was now summoning them. They were needed.

And if Parcival could just get Pike out of this bar without further incident, they would be able to respond. Parcival tapped a small button on his wrist unit to indicate "message received," and then he said to Pike in an urgent whisper, "Pike. We just got an important call. We'd better get out of here."

Out of the side of his mouth, Pike said, "Understood." And then in a louder voice he said, "Tell you what, Runya. Just to show that everything is square, you keep the racing craft. I'm not much for life in the fast space lanes anyway. Besides, you would have wanted it that way."

"Well, that's . . . that's darned decent of me," said Runya, more confused than he could recall ever having been in his life.

Parcival jabbed him urgently. "Pike, let's go already."

"Right." Parcival stuck out a hand. "No hard feelings."

Runya took the proffered hand and shook it extremely vigorously. Pike started to stammer out, "Not so hard," but he was too slow.

Half a dozen playing cards slid out of Pike's sleeve.

Parcival covered his eyes for a moment, "Oh, boy."

It took Runya a couple of seconds to realize what had just happened. Then, with a roar, he reached for a huge blaster that hung on his side. He had an equally huge blaster on the other side.

Before it was cleared of its holster, Pike swung one of his huge feet upward. The kick caught Runya deep in the pit of his stomach. Automatically Runya doubled over, gasping, and Parcival stepped forward, swinging his bat with all his strength.

Anticipating the blow even in his pain, Runya angled his shoulders and managed to avoid the full impact. Nevertheless, the bat managed to drive consciousness from Runya's right head.

Parcival raised his bat again but Runya swept out with one massive arm, knocking Parcival off his feet. With surprising strength Pike grabbed Parcival and hauled him up. "Let's go, little buddy," Pike urged. "Discretion and all that."

"Good idea, Pike," said Parcival. Grabbing his bat tightly he followed Pike out of bar. The crowd parted to make way for them as they held their respective hats in front of them, both filled to the brim with Pike's winnings.

Runya tried to stagger to his feet. However, since Parcival had managed to incapacitate Runya's right head, this served to put out of commission the entire right side of Runya's body. As a result his three huge right arms hung uselessly at his side, about as threatening as oven mitts. His right leg was a stick. His left leg, arm and head were all still alive and kicking. He hauled himself up to his one good leg and howled after Pike, "Get back here, coward!"

He tried to stagger after them and lurched wildly from side to side, looking like a fish out of water. He would

take one large step with his left leg, and then futilely haul
his sleeping leg after him.

He shook a fist in the air. "Coward!" he shouted again.
"Come back and take your death like a Foppo!" He lurched
forward again and this time fell flat on his face. "Someone
help me up!" he raged, but all the sentient beings in the
bar moved back. He had beaten them all at cards at one
time or another, and as a result had not earned himself any
friends.

Furious, he reached around with his one good arm and
slapped his other head as hard as he could. His other head
groaned low in his throat. "Wake up, you moron!"
howled Runya, and his other head came to half-wakefulness.
Enough for Runya to get the other leg operating. He stood
again, still limping but now with more speed, and barrelled through the swinging doors of the bar.

And tripped over the drunken Hush.

He fell badly and smacked the still-groggy head on the
ground. It was enough to send it straight back to dream-
land and the livid Runya flailed about helplessly on top of
the pinned Hush.

"Piiiike!" he screamed. "I'll get you for this. I'll get
you if I have to follow you to the edge of the universe and
back again. You'll pay for this indignity. So help me,
you'll pay!"

His voice echoed in Pike's head even as the Photon
Warrior entered the *Zephyr*, Parcival right behind him.
"Shut the hatch, Parcival," he called. Parcival ran to the
control board at the helm, pressed an array of buttons and
breathed a sigh of relief as he watched the door swing
upward and snugly close. They were secure. Nothing could
breech the hull now.

He turned and let out a yelp.

Runya was standing directly in front of them, both
heads conscious, lifting all four arms back. He smashed on
the front of the ship and a tremor shook the entire space
vehicle.

"Let's get out of here!" said Pike, grabbing a helm seat and powering up. A hum filled the entire ship and Parcival quickly punched in coordinates. The *Zephyr* roared to full life, and roaring as well was Runya. To Parcival he sounded like an angry cement mixer.

"Punch it, Parcival," called Pike.

Parcival nodded, all business, tearing his eyes away from the raging alien directly in front of him, separated only by the unbreakable view window. "We're out of here," he said. "Immediate vertical lift-off, three, two one . . ."

The ship rose off the launching pad several feet, and then stopped. It shook, as if anchored, and Parcival and Pike craned forward.

"He's keeping us down!" said Pike incredulously.

Parcival shook his head, unperturbed. They were in his realm now . . . no gambling, no games of skill and deception. This was pure logic, and logic and data indicated that there was no conceivable way that Runya could prevent *Zephyr* from lift-off. "He's not keeping us anywhere," said Parcival evenly, and brought full power on line.

Runya was forced to release the ship, and it soared above his head. But already having lost his grip on his prey, Runya was undeterred. He bolted across the landing field to his own racing space hopper and jumped into the small cockpit.

As *Zephyr* leaped heavenward, the atmosphere already thinning and the lights of the stars beckoning, Parcival turned towards Pike. There was a hint of scolding in his bespectacled eyes. "Pike . . . were you cheating in that game?"

"Now, now," said Pike. "Just because you saw a few extra cards, don't assume that I was using them."

"Don't snow me, Pike."

"I wouldn't dream of it, little buddy," said Pike mildly. "I played that game on the up-and-up. I just always keep a few extra cards with me. Just in case."

"Uh huh," said Parcival, not entirely convinced.

Abruptly a small light began to flash. "Someone's on our tail," observed Parcival.

"I wonder who that could be?" said Pike drily.

"I don't care if it's the *Starship Enterprise*," said Parcival. "We're not sticking around." He locked in the coordinates for Intellistar, the home and headquarters of the Photon Alliance, and said, "Hang on to your spare cards, Pike."

Zephyr leaped forward and space warped and twisted around it. In less than a second they had jumped into hyperspace, untraceable and uncatchable.

Runya's space hopper circled futilely in the place where the *Zephyr* had just been. Roaring his anger, Runya shouted, "I'll get you, Pike. You'll be food for carrion eaters before I'm done with you. You can run, Pike, but you can't hide. I'll be after you, no matter how long it takes. That's a promise, Pike. That's a promise."

2

School Daze

Christopher Jarvis stared at the test paper in front of him and felt the entire book of *A Tale of Two Cities* swimming before his eyes.

He stared again at the cross-match in front of him as he tried to massage an answer from his fevered brain. Now who had said, " 'Tis a far far better thing I do now . . ."? It was from the end of the book, but . . .

The teenager glanced surreptitiously around his class. The teacher, Miss Mednitsky, circled the class like a hawk. An attractive young woman, she nevertheless had an incredible air of menace when it came time to watch for cheating during one of her English Lit classes.

She stopped next to Chris's desk for a moment and stared down at him. Chris looked up at her ingratiatingly and waved his eyebrows. Her mouth twitched slightly and she silently pointed a long finger at the test paper. Chris nodded and bent his head back to work.

As she walked away, Chris glanced across the aisle to his pal, Al Fedder. Al was filling out the answers with brisk certainty, and Chris was both surprised and envious. Al was not usually any particular whiz when it came to scholastics, although when it came to car engines, no one could touch his proficiency. Chris had been studying for this test and he knew Al hadn't. Yet here Chris was wrestling with the examination and Al was clearly undeterred by any of the questions.

Then he saw Al look up cautiously, and when Al was certain that Miss Mednitsky was not watching, he pulled a $5'' \times 7''$ index card from under his sweater and consulted it. He glanced from the card to his paper, quickly made a correction on his paper and tucked the card back into hiding.

Chris realized that his mouth was hanging open and quickly shut it. Al noticed Chris staring at him and winked broadly.

"Chris."

His head snapped around. Miss Mednitsky was looking at him curiously through her large, round glasses. "Is Al's test more interesting than yours?"

More right than mine, Chris thought privately. Out loud, he said, "No, Miss Mednitsky."

"Then let's keep eyes front, shall we?"

He nodded and hunched back over his test, and this time made certain not to look anywhere but down.

Al was going through his locker when he felt a tap on his shoulder. He turned and grinned lopsidedly. Al was tall and gangling, a head taller than Chris. "Hey, some test, wasn't that, Chris?"

"Some of us had less problems than others," said Chris. In addition to being shorter than Al, Chris was a little broader in the shoulders, a little more muscular. He and Al had first met back in grade school, having gotten into a fist fight over something that neither of them could now recall. When the fight had ended and they'd both been lying there, bruised and cut up, they decided that they were going to be best friends. And so it had remained through their school career.

Chris leaned against a locker and said, "What did you think you were doing before?"

"Passing the test," said Al easily.

"Man, how could you do that?"

"What, you mean not offer you the answers?" Al tossed his books in the locker and shut the door, spinning the combo to relock it. "Come on. I know you too well, Chris. You'd never go for something like that."

"It's wrong, Al," said Chris. "You know it's wrong."

Al shrugged expansively and started to walk down the hallway. Around them kids bustled about, for school had ended and everyone was eager to get home. Chris fell into step next to him.

"Look, Chris, all I know is that when I get out of this joint for good, I'm going to be working for Tony Driscoll down at his service station, and eventually I'm going to be the most highly paid mechanic in the Valley. I'll probably have my own place someday, and Miss Mednitsky will bring her overheating Pontiac to me and beg me to fix it, and then who'll be on top? And I ask you, where does Charles Dickens fit into all of that, huh?"

Chris shrugged. "Nowhere, I guess. But the point is—"

"The point is, Chris, that my folks'll give me grief if I flunk Mednitsky's class, and grief over something that I'll never have any use for, like *A Tale of Two Cities* or *Silas Marner* or any of that other garbage, is grief that I just don't need. *Kapeesh*, buddy?"

"I suppose," sighed Chris.

"So look, promise you'll keep mum about it?" said Al, and he turned to face his old friend. "Won't breath a word about it?"

Chris pulled an imaginary zipper across his mouth and Al grinned broadly. "Awright!" he said, and then he draped an arm around Chris's shoulders and dropped his

voice to a confidential tone. "Wanna have some fun
tonight?"

Chris raised an eyebrow. "What've you got in mind?"

Al made a great show of looking left and right, as if
concerned that they were under observation. Then he whispered. "My folks are out of town. I can take the Porsche
and pick you up at seven, and we can go out and pick up
some girls. Girls are suckers for a Porsche." He intoned
gravely, "There is no substitute."

"You're crazy. I mean, that is the worst idea I've ever
heard you come up with."

Al was taken aback. "You got something against girls?"

"No! But don't you see? You can get in all kinds of
trouble. Remember what happened last time you took your
parents' car, when they were out of town?"

"I told you," said Al with infinite patience, "I never
would have hit that thing if it hadn't leaped into my way."

"A tree, Al. You hit a tree. A tree leaped into your
way?"

Al shrugged. "I didn't say it was a very smart tree."

Chris took Al by the shoulders and shook him as if
trying to shake sense into him. "Al, you're seventeen.
You've just gotten a license. You don't want to lose it.
Now, last time you swiped your parents' car and wrapped it
around a tree, you ran home and told the cops it had been
stolen. How many times do you think you're going to get
away with that?"

"It's not going to happen again," Al told him. "I'm a
lot better driver now than I was then. You can't compare it.
Okay, Chris, bottom line here. Are you in or out?"

He shook his head. "Out, Al. Besides, we have a test
coming up in social studies, and some of us have to study."

"Okay, that's cool. But you'll keep your mouth shut for
me, won't you?"

Chris hesitated. He was really concerned that Al was
going to get himself killed. But Al seemed so confident in
himself. Maybe he was right. That earlier incident had

been almost a year ago; they had practically been kids. His father practiced driving with him, and he had indeed gotten a lot better. Besides, it was his neck on the line, not Chris's. If keeping quiet for Al would preserve their friendship, it wasn't really all that big a deal.

Was it?

"If you find a really good babe, see if she has a sister for me," said Chris.

Al smiled broadly and high-fived him. "Catch you on the rebound, Chris," he said.

At that moment the ring Chris wore, set with a purple stone, began to flash. He quickly jammed it in his pocket and said, "I'm out of here, too. And be sure to drive carefully, you cluck."

"Hey! People call me Mr. Cautious."

"Only people who don't know you the way I do."

Moments later Chris was on his bicycle and pedalling furiously across town to the Photon Center.

Whereas before he had been thinking about his friend, now his mind was solely on whatever task might be waiting for him.

It was remarkable. Not too long ago, he had been an ordinary teenager who frequently would engage in his favorite pastime—Photon, frequently called the ultimate game on Earth. The Photon Center, towards which Chris was now furiously pedalling, was a large unassuming building that housed a mazelike arena. There, players on a Red team and players on a Green team, clad in helmets and equipped with futuristic guns that fired beams of light, would hunt each other and the teams' respective goals during a six-minute playing period. The object was to zap your opponent's equipment into inactivity while avoiding being hit yourself. You also received extra points by nailing the opposing team's goal.

Of all the warriors who stalked the maze of the local Photon Center, the best had been Chris. Except when he played, he was no longer Christopher Jarvis but took on the name Bhodi Li. As Bhodi Li, he had had many games and many challenges, and no one had been able to top him.

But that was before he had encountered the biggest challenge of his life. When his score had leaped over 2500, time all over the planet Earth had frozen, and Bhodi Li had found himself whisked uncounted millions of miles from Earth to a far-off bio-mechanical space station named Intellistar. And there—

He forced his concentration back to the present as he arrived at the Photon Center and smoothly slid his bicycle into the waiting rack.

The crowd was just starting to build at the Photon Center, since school had just let out. Several of the regulars greeted Chris cheerfully and he waved back even as he went to the preparation center and buckled on the power pack, helmet and Photon phaser. Then he took his place with the Red Team and waited eagerly for the match in progress to be over so that he could get in and get himself transported to his waiting fellow Photon Guardians.

He took a moment to survey the other players standing nearby. The teams were not preset—whoever showed up played, and team assignments were made randomly. He wondered how each of the others around him would have fared if it had been they, instead of he, who had been chosen for the responsibility of being a Photon Guardian. A certain amount of vanity made him feel that, of everyone here, he was indisputably the best qualified.

The great doors in front of him opened, and he and the rest of the Red team were led over to the far end of the carpeted arena. As if I need to be led, thought Chris smugly, since he knew every step of the way, every inch of the entire arena. Still, he could tell from the dazed looks of some of the players next to him that there were a couple of neos out here. Too bad he wasn't here to really play this time around—if there were this many novices on the opposing team, he could have racked up big points. But if there was one thing that Chris Jarvis, a.k.a. Bhodi Li, had learned, it was that there were more important things in life than playing games.

The game began and both teams started running toward each other's goals. Bhodi was leading the pack, an uncanny sixth sense enabling him to dodge the blasts of the other players almost without looking.

Within seconds he was standing before the goal of the other team. Suddenly his inner sense warned him, and he turned, firing without even stopping to take aim. There was an opposing player there, hiding in the shadows, who had been waiting to pick off anyone who tried to shoot the goal. But he had reckoned without the uncanny reflexes of Bhodi Li, and the would-be ambusher found himself without power for the requisite five seconds after being shot.

More than enough time. Bhodi Li turned, aimed his phaser at the goal and called out, "The Light shines."

The player who had been hit said, "What do you mean, the—" and then he ground to a halt, frozen in midsentence. All around Bhodi Li the sounds of game play halted, and Bhodi knew that MOM, the super-computer of Intellistar, was at work.

A cone of blue light issued from the goal and bathed him in its glow. He felt the power surge through him, felt his muscles becoming stronger and more powerful. His ordinary clothes were replaced by his Photon uniform—red trousers and white chest rig, all heavily padded to protect him from random blasts. His arms were padded as well, and he felt energy flowing into his phaser. Instead of harmless beams of light that registered on a chest plate, he now held a working phaser that was capable of slicing through titanium with ease.

Then the world turned sideways and Bhodi Li's molecules leaped into space.

3

Gambler

Every time Bhodi Li looked upon his teammates, he was always tempted to hand them small candy bars and tell them how good they looked in their trick-or-treat costumes.

As Bhodi stepped into the central briefing room of Intellistar, the field of stars twinkling merrily in the blackness of space right outside the window, Leon was the first to greet him. Leon was the powerbase of the Photon Guardians. A huge lizardlike being, Leon's friendly outgoing nature was superseded by only two things—his fierceness in battle and his great physical strength. On his shoulder he wore a phaser bazooka the size of an MX missile. Leon was fond of saying that he could pick off an orbiting enemy cruiser while standing on a planet surface, and for all Bhodi knew, Leon was correct.

Lord Baethan and Tivia were deep in discussion and didn't even take note of Bhodi's presence at first. Lord Baethan was a gleaming cyborg, and was, in addition to being a formidable warrior, the team's wizard. Whenever the Guardians needed the equivalent of a rabbit out of the hat to save them, they turned to Baethan to pull it off. Somehow he always did.

Tivia was a self-assured young woman, about Bhodi's age, from a planet where warrior women were the dominant group. Tivia peered out at the world over a mask that obscured the lower half of her face. However, Bhodi had recently seen her unmasked briefly and had been surprised by just how attractive she was. Of course he wouldn't let on about it, just as he wouldn't let on how attracted to her he was. It was kind of an unspoken agreement with them, for although Bhodi believed Tivia was attracted to him as well, she preferred to treat him in the same high-handed manner she treated all men. The general consensus among the Photon Guardians was that Bhodi and Tivia would either wind up in each other's arms or kill each other. In addition to the fascination she held for Bhodi, Tivia was also the group's hand-to-hand-combat expert. She was unrelenting and fierce in battle and had bailed Bhodi out of more than one tight situation.

Over in another corner were Parcival and Pike. They were also in deep discussion, and Bhodi sensed that something was up with them. Well, he wasn't concerned. Even if they had a disagreement with each other, it wouldn't last long. Since he had no family outside of Photon, Parcival looked upon Pike as practically the father he never had. Bhodi had never quite understood why, because Pike was such an odd-looking creature that he couldn't comprehend how Parcival could see him as a father substitute.

Parcival was the group's computer expert and information whiz. It was Parcival who gathered all the raw data that the Photon Warriors needed and who developed the most workable plan for any situation. Only the incomparable Lord Baethan exceeded Parcival in strategy planning, since Baethan's emotionless cyborg state enabled him to view any tough spot dispassionately.

Pike was ideal for subterfuge. The resident con artist, capable of talking his way out of situations when brute force was either inappropriate or insufficient, Pike was also a shape shifter, capable of transforming himself into any creature roughly his mass.

"Photon Guardians, please come to order," said a soft female voice that immediately commanded their attention.

Bhodi looked up, and there was the soft, gleaming outline of MOM on the wall. The super-computer was most visible as an array of lights vaguely in the shape of a female head, but all of Intellistar was actually part of the bio-mechanoid creature that was MOM, first and greatest of the Photon Guardians.

They lined up in front of her as she spoke, her voice issuing from everywhere and nowhere at the same time. "I have located someone whom I feel can be a great asset to us," said MOM.

"All right!" said Bhodi. "I won't be the new kid on the block anymore."

"Don't worry, Bhodi," said Tivia soothingly. "To me, you'll always be the brash, arrogant young man you were when you first got here."

"Gee, thanks," he said unenthusiastically.

Leon and Pike glanced at each other with a "Here we go again" look.

"Bhodi, Tivia, please," said MOM. "Here is my new candidate for membership among the Photon Guardians."

MOM's viewscreen blanked for a moment, and then a new image came onto the screen.

Bhodi Li grinned. There were some differences, a few curves of alien design, but he was clearly looking at a Photon Center. Here was a familiar and pleasing sight. There was a game in action and Bhodi was surprised to see that they were not wearing helmets. Instead they wore headbands of red or green, made from some material that looked like plastic but probably was not. Extending from the headband in each case was a round piece that covered the right ear like half an ear muff. Otherwise the battery belts, the chest plates and the phasers were identical to Bhodi's own.

Another major difference was the players themselves.

They were humanoids, meaning that they had two arms, two legs, a head, and opposable thumbs. But all of them had skin that was dark blue, so dark that it was hard to keep track of them even on the monitor. Their hair was slightly lighter blue than their skin, and their eyes were round, pupilless, and scarlet.

"This is the planet Kenilwurth," MOM was saying. "And this is the potential candidate."

Her monitor focused on one player for a moment, but only for a moment. For within the next moment he had disappeared from the screen.

"Where'd he go?" asked Pike.

"Obvious," Tivia spoke up. "They have some sort of invisibility power."

"I'm afraid you're wrong, Tivia."

At MOM's correction, Bhodi Li moaned. "Tivia's wrong. I can die now. I've finally seen it all."

Tivia archly chose to ignore Bhodi's remark.

The picture on the monitor moved around and caught up with the player. He had an intensity on his face that Bhodi recognized as what he imagined he looked like caught up in playing Photon.

The Photon Guardians watched in amazement as the potential recruit went through his paces. It was nothing short of astonishing. He moved so quickly that a number of times MOM had to recalibrate in order to find him again. No one even came close to zapping him, and in the meantime he was so laughably beyond everyone else out on the arena floor that it was ludicrous.

For a moment the competitive blood surged in Bhodi, and he hungered to get out there and take the recruit on, one-on-one. Then he remonstrated with himself that there were more serious considerations here than game playing.

"Remarkable," breathed Tivia, and Bhodi glanced over

at her. She was watching the screen with rapt fascination, and Bhodi couldn't help but feel a pang of jealousy. He wondered if, when the Photon Guardians had first viewed Bhodi Li himself, in considering him for membership in their ranks, Tivia had expressed that kind of amazement at his own battle prowess. Somehow he had a feeling she hadn't.

"What's his name, MOM?" asked Parcival.

"His name on Kenilwurth is Jwwsquezyt," she said.

"Boy, I know a hundred guys with that name," said Bhodi.

"Really?" said Parcival. "Is that all? I know of an entire planet where everybody has that name."

He spoke with such a deadpan that Bhodi couldn't tell if he was kidding or not.

"However," MOM was saying, "his Photon name translates as Gambler."

Leon nodded approvingly. "My kind of name," he said in his gravelly voice. "A young pup who's not afraid to take a few chances here and there. We need some adventurous spirit in the group—no offense, Bhodi."

Bhodi nodded, suddenly unsure if no longer being the novice in the group was such a good thing.

They watched him for a few more moments, dazzled by his agility, his speed and his fearlessness. At one point he somersaulted between two opposing players, getting them to zap each other in their futile attempts to hit him, and Bhodi stifled a laugh at the sheer audacity of the maneuver. You had to admire this guy—he had enough nerve for an entire armada of Photon Guardians.

"I'm convinced," said Bhodi. "Bring him up."

"My sentiments exactly," said Leon.

Parcival was making quick calculations on his wrist computer. "My computations show that the odds against Gambler ever being hit, based on his current performance, are 1,827,526.3 to 1. I see no way in which we can refuse to take him on."

"His skill is remarkable for one with no formal training," said Baethan in his cold, almost mechanical voice. "I vote we appoint him to our ranks."

"Absolutely," said Pike. "He's quick, smart and obviously has a lot on the ball."

There was a silence, and they all turned to the one Photon Guardian who had not said anything.

Tivia was watching his every move and was slowly shaking her head. "There's something about him I don't trust," she said.

Bhodi sighed. "There's something about all males you don't trust," he said. "Why don't you put aside these silly prejudices of yours and judge people on their merits, not their gender."

"That's what I am doing," she said pointedly. "And there's something about him that just doesn't feel right, gender aside. Still, if all of you are so gung ho on him, I'll waive any objections I have, since there's nothing I can really point to and say, 'This is what makes me nervous about him.' Although, MOM, I do wish that we could have at least one other female member."

"I do try to be attentive to all potential candidates," MOM said primly. "Sex, as we all agree, is not important."

"Now, I wouldn't say that," Bhodi said, and he was about to continue except Tivia's dirty look cut him off.

"I'm bringing him up to Intellistar," said MOM. "Get ready, everyone."

Bhodi watched the screen and couldn't help but laugh to himself as he saw the expression on Gambler's face. All around him, the other players in the arena had frozen into immobility. At first he clearly thought that it was some sort of trick to make him an easier target, but when he saw one player frozen in midleap, he dismissed that idea extremely quickly. Then a cone of blue light surrounded him, and Gambler was whisked off the viewscreen.

"Here he comes," said Leon, and sure enough within seconds Gambler had materialized in front of them.

His back was to them as he looked around, completely confused and befuddled. Bhodi felt a twinge of sympathy for him. It seemed all too recently that Bhodi himself had been the recruit. He remembered how difficult it had been to accept what his senses were telling him, and how his initial impulse had been to back out of the responsibility that was being thrust upon him. So he was prepared to be as sympathetic as possible to all the conflicting emotions and struggles that Gambler would be certain to encounter in the days and weeks ahead.

Gambler suddenly sensed their presence and spun, so fast that he almost tripped himself up. He had been unprepared for the burst of speed his Photon-charged body would give him. But, to his credit, he corrected this almost immediately.

He turned slowly and looked at the array of beings in front of him. Then slowly, incredulously, a smile spread across his face. "Faaaar out," he said.

Bhodi was stunned. He had expected a reaction similar to his own, but this new fellow, Gambler, seemed hardly thrown at all.

"Where am I?" he asked. "Spatial coordinate."

"That is not relevant," MOM said briskly. "Welcome to the Light, Gambler of Kenilwurth."

He looked at each of them, his gaze resting for the longest on Tivia. He seemed to be memorizing every inch of her shapely figure clad in its silver and yellow mesh armor. Bhodi could not tell what Tivia, under her mask, was doing, whether she was smiling or frowning at this open attention.

Gambler looked away from her and at MOM. "What's the light, sprite? Aside from the obvious meanings."

Leon lumbered forward. "She means welcome to the Photon Alliance, Gambler."

"Photon?" said Gambler. "Photon's a game, a harmless pastime that helps me make a few bucks on the side, Clyde."

"It is far more than that, Gambler," rumbled Lord Baethan. "Photon is life."

Gambler laughed. His voice was light but not insubstantial. He rested his weight on one leg, holding his phaser in a relaxed manner. "That sounds real nice. Care to run past me exactly what you're talking about?"

Bhodi Li was suddenly aware of Tivia at his side. In a low whisper she said, "He's even more insufferable than *you* were."

Deep down he had begun to agree with her, but because of her criticism he felt instantly compelled to disagree with her. "Give the guy a break," he muttered. "He's probably scared as anything, and he's talking a good show to cover it."

"We'll see," she said.

And then Leon started to launch into the speech that he had given Bhodi when Bhodi was first brought into the Alliance. For one moment Bhodi had a mental picture of a large recruitment poster with Leon pointing fiercely saying, "Uncle Leon wants you to join the Photon Guardians." He stifled a laugh.

"In the beginning," Leon said reverently, "there was Photon, the crystal energy that brought life to the entire universe. Some great cataclysm caused the Photon energy to shatter, creating a light and dark universe. These two universes are constantly struggling for control. We, the Photon Warriors, are the Guardians of the Light."

Leon waved, and in front of him a hologram of a round Photon crystal materialized. The clear globe sparkled before him, glistening with the light of life. "If," said Leon, "any of us energizes a Photon crystal, it fills the planet it's on with positive light—green, glowing beauty . . . in short, life."

"You said there was a dark universe," said Gambler. He was leaning against a console with easy familiarity, as if he'd been there for years and years.

Leon nodded approvingly. "You're listening, all right.

The Dark Universe is ruled over by the Warlord of Arr and his six evil henchmen. They want to spread the threat of darkness throughout our universe. They too can energize Photon crystals, except that theirs spread darkness throughout a planet. Nothing good can exist there, and it becomes a haven for evil. Whoever energizes a planet has influence over that planet for a hundred years.''

Gambler nodded in understanding. ''And you want me to join you in the Photon Alliance. That's it in a nutshell.''

''Yes, but it's a pretty big nutshell,'' said Leon.

''True, but I understand the responsibility. However''—he bowed his head slightly—''I must decline.''

Bhodi half smiled. He had been expecting this. It was exactly the reaction he had first had. This wasn't his fight, this was nothing he wanted to get involved in. Photon was a harmless amusement, not something he wanted to devote his life to. It had taken him a little time to come around, but eventually he had. Obviously Gambler was going to need that same time for reconsideration.

But Tivia was on her feet. ''Why must you decline?'' she said imperiously, her tone suggesting that he had better answer her immediately.

Gambler looked at her with his great scarlet eyes and said, ''Because I am clearly unworthy of being in such august company.''

The lights on MOM's console sparkled. ''What?''

''You beings—you Photon Guardians—are beings of great skill and talent. I'm simply not in your league. I have a certain amount of flash and ability, I guess, but nothing in your power class. I don't see how you can possibly think that I'm deserving to be in your rank.''

There was a stunned silence. Then Pike said, ''We were watching you in action, Gambler. From what we saw, you need take a back seat to no one.''

''Well, I'm very flattered you feel that way, sir. Of course I've heard of the Photon Alliance—Great Kolker,'' he swore, ''how could anyone not have heard of the

Photon Alliance? But in my backwater little planet, it was more in the nature of fairy tales and myths than anything else. I had always thought that the Photon Centers were just created by people who wanted to cash in on the legend of Photon bravery.''

"*I* created the Photon Centers," said MOM, "as a means of testing the inhabitants of certain planets and to see who had the greatest potential to become Photon Guardians.''

Gambler sniffled, apparently overwhelmed by the moment. "This . . . this is an honor that I would not have believed possible." He grabbed Leon's head on either side and shook it. "Thank you," he said fervently.

"Why are you shaking my head?" asked Leon, who felt his brains being scrambled.

"It's the custom on my planet." He quickly withdrew his hands and said, "Sorry."

"Oh, that's okay," said Leon as he wobbled slightly. "Gotta respect other folks' customs."

"How about this instead?" suggested Bhodi, sticking out a hand. When Gambler simply stared at it, Bhodi took Gambler's hand, stuck it in his own and then shook it firmly.

Gambler grinned. "Say, this isn't bad. Thanks . . ." He paused.

"Bhodi Li."

Gambler suddenly stepped back, struck with a sudden thought. "Wait. *The* Bhodi Li? Of course. This is all just too fantastic. You're a legend."

Bhodi grinned around at the others. "Hear that? I'm a legend in my own time."

"Or at least a legend in your own mind," said Tivia, but Bhodi wasn't impressed by any put-downs at this point. He was too busy flying high, and he knew that he and Gambler were going to be getting on just great.

4

First Mission

The two ships cut across the blackness of space, eerily silent, and no one would have realized that what they were witnessing was a race of life and death.

The smaller ship was a class D freighter belonging to the Emperor of the planet Dekka, and at that moment the freighter pilot (and sole occupant) was primarily concerned with staying alive.

The grizzled Captain Burnside, for such was the pilot's name, checked the sensors and cursed long and fluently. The pursuing ship was right on his tail and didn't seem to show the least interest in getting off his back. He did not even have to see the markings to realize that this was a ship belonging to the Warlord of Arr. Nor did he have to be a genius to figure out just what it was that the crew of the Arrian ship wanted from him. They wanted his cargo, but he would be burned in the sun of Andromeda before he let those villainous scum take what he had hidden in the bowels of his ship.

He cursed the luck that had allowed the Arrian attack

ship to sneak up on him and take him unawares. And he was doubly furious that, before he had even known what was happening, they had gotten off a shot that had crippled his star drive. It had been such a short trip back to Dekka, and he'd decided to take it in a leisurely fashion. Well, he was paying for his leisure now, because they'd caught him in normal space and nailed him really well. And just what in the twenty-eight worlds was he going to do now?

A voice came over his subspace radio. "Dekkan ship," came the voice of one of the Warlord's Soldarrs, "surrender your cargo or we will blow you out of space."

He thought of ignoring them, but then something in his defiant nature made him punch on the hailing frequency. "Big talk, Soldarr," snarled Burnside. "If you wanted to blow me up, you could have done it by now. But you're not going to until you get my cargo, and that I can promise you you won't do."

There was silence for a moment. Then, "Very well. You have brought this on yourself."

Knowing what was coming, Burnside madly grabbed the controls and tried to swerve his craft to one side. His bald head gleamed with perspiration, his red and yellow headband soaking through. Seconds later an incredible impact against the side of his ship told him that the superior fire power of the Arrian ship had cut through his deflectors with laughable ease. His ship lurched and he skidded, almost losing his balance on the cramped deck. He grabbed his command chair and snarled more invectives at the Arrians, cursing out their entire family trees.

Off to starboard he saw a planet, dark and uninviting. He didn't even have to glance at his starcharts to know off the top of his head that it was the planet simply designated M172. He guided his crippled ship towards it, hoping against hope that he could make planetfall. Even as he did, he scanned his instrument board and cursed. Energy was severely depleted.

On his rear scanner he saw the Arrian ship looming over

him. They weren't going to let him make it to the planet. They would blow him to bits rather than chance his escaping with his precious cargo. As long as he had any energy left, there was a chance that he—

Then he hit on a desperate move. He started flipping switches and within moments he cut all his energy. He killed forward motion and then, taking a deep breath, he even cut life support. Within minutes, he knew, the air would become stale and unbreathable, the temperature in his ship matching the coldness of space's vacuum. But he had no choice.

He waited, and prayed that he wasn't making a mistake.

A minute passed, then two.

He watched out his front viewing port, even having killed the energy to the monitor. His ship was adrift and slowly it turned and faced the Arrian ship that hovered kilometers away.

There was a sudden thud, but it was not accompanied by any flash of light. They had not fired at him. He realized with a leap of hope that they had done what he wanted. They had placed a tractor beam on him and were planning to pull him into the ship.

He waited, not daring to breathe as he drew closer and closer to the Arrian ship.

It all came down, he realized as his fingers hovered above his weapons systems, to what you know versus what you don't know. They thought he was helpless. They thought his energy was gone. They didn't know that he had a few dregs left. And what he, Burnside, knew, was that in order to use the tractor beam, the Arrian ship had to drop its shields.

Closer. Closer. One chance at this. The Soldarrs were not bright, but if he blew it this time, he would not be getting a second chance.

Closer.

Closer, until it filled his entire viewing port, until it

seemed that all of space was gone and that only the dark Arrian craft was there.

Now.

Burnside keyed in all the energy he had left. It was a power surge that the Soldarrs would detect, but he prayed that they would read it as a last-ditch attempt to break free of their tractor beam.

The Arrian ship took form on his targeting computer, a bright green outline. An X appeared on the optimum target—their engine room.

"I hate Soldarrs," muttered Burnside, and he stabbed down on the fire button.

For a split instant nothing happened, and Burnside thought he had miscalculated the amount of energy he had left. Then his ship lurched and a bolt of lambent energy shot forth from his ship's cannons.

It hit the Arrian ship square on target. The great warship shuddered down its length, and then an explosion ripped the hull outward. Air rushed out and space rushed in, and Burnside felt his ship break loose from the tractor beam. Kicking in the last of his energy, he moved away from the Arrian warship. But he was slow, plodding. He felt like a sick, ponderous animal as he creeped away from the crippled Arrian ship.

And then, pieces flying in every direction, the Arrian warship blew up.

There are no shockwaves in space or else Burnside's ship would have been torn apart by the impact. But fragments shot out everywhere and Burnside urged his ship forward, frantic that his hull might be breached and that he, ironically, might meet the same fate that he had just delivered to the shipload of Soldarrs. His only wish was that the Warlord himself were on the ship, but he knew that the Warlord never left his hideous main base, Scarrcastle.

M172 loomed before him. He quickly realized that he had nowhere near enough energy to leap into hyperspace and complete his journey to Dekka. He would run dry of energy in that faster-than-light realm, and that would certainly be the finish for him. He only had one option—to use what energy he had left to guide himself into as soft a landing as possible.

He also did the one other thing he could. He brought up his subspace radio and started calling for help.

Captain Burnside was a proud man, but even he knew when he was in need of help.

In the darkest reaches of the universe sat the Scarrcastle, a dark structure radiating evil. It was so evil that to reach it you didn't travel light-years, you traveled dark-years.

The Scarrcastle looked like an explosion of an atom bomb, frozen into hideous permanence. It bristled with armaments and ships, Dark Destroyers as they were known in some parts of the universe. It sucked in all light that came its way, but it didn't simply pull in the light. It captured it, twisted it into something unclean and sent it back out to commit atrocities.

Deep in the heart of the Scarrcastle was the Warlord's inner sanctum. He rarely left it but instead sat there like a dark spider, huge and monstrous.

Now standing before him were his six Dark Guardians. Their origins were cloaked in mystery. Some said that they had somehow sprung straight from the evil of the Warlord himself. Others said that they had all once been benevolent beings, captured one by one and twisted to the evil machinations of the Warlord. In the end it really didn't matter. They were there to do the Warlord's bidding, and they aided in spreading his dark power throughout the universe.

The six of them—Warriarr, Pirarr, Mandarr, Destructarr, Bugarr and Dogarr—stood before their master. They always faced him with a mixture of anticipation and dread. The Warlord was quicksilver in his moods. Sometimes he would send them out to perform evil deeds in his name, and that was the sort of thing they lived for. But other times something had not gone right, and the Warlord searched for someone on whom he could vent his wrath. It was those times that death seemed an option that might not be such a bad idea.

Mandarr took a step forward. He was human in appearance, for indeed he had once been an Earthling. His eyes were covered with a dark mask, and into his head were plugged wires that helped keep him firmly in thrall of the Warlord. "What do you wish of us, my Lord?"

The chilling voice echoed through the chamber. "A transport ship from the planet Dekka, carrying a cargo of pure Photonium, has been forced down onto planet M172."

"I am not familiar with that planet, my Lord," said Mandarr.

"M172 was once an inhabited planet," said the Warlord. "Millennia ago, the population wiped itself out through global warfare. It was"—there was a pause that was almost wistful—"it was gratifying."

There was a silence then, and the Dark Guardians wisely chose not to intrude on the thoughts of the Warlord. At length he continued, "A warship of incompetent Soldarrs allowed themselves to be outmaneuvered by the freighter and, quite justifiably, were blown out of space for it. However, the freighter was depleted of energy and forced to set down on the planet. The captain showed great resourcefulness and skill. If possible, capture him alive. He could be converted into a valuable Soldarr. Otherwise do what you must. The first imperative is to capture the Photonium. In its raw form, before it is converted into Photon crystals, it has power enough for me to conquer the entire universe. Power enough to wipe away the blot of the Photon Guardians for all time. This is too important for just two or three of you. I want you all to go. Mandarr, you are in command of this expedition."

Mandarr bowed slightly, as did the others, "Thank you, my Lord." He raised a fist, as did the others. "Let the Darkness grow."

All of the Dark Guardians slumped foward and, issuing forth from them, came their projectons. Projectons were holographic projections of the Dark Guardians, but they had weight and form and substance. They were just as deadly as their real counterparts, and they couldn't be killed.

They repeated again, "Let the Darkness grow," and then turned to board the warship that would transport them to M172, and their prize of pure Photonium.

Behind them in the darkness, the Warlord laughed.

"I still don't like him."

Bhodi and Tivia were watching Gambler sparring with Baethan. It had been several weeks since Gambler had been brought up to Intellistar, and in that time Bhodi had come and gone several times during Gambler's training period. Rather than thrust a raw recruit into the heat of battle, Gambler had been making repeated visits to Intellistar and worked out with the Photon Warriors in turns, learning what he could. Now, as with incredible agility he dodged a blast from Lord Baethan's staff, Gambler was showing again and again why he deserved to be part of the Photon Alliance.

"Why don't you like him?" demanded Bhodi, surprised at Tivia's attitude.

"He's too smooth," said Tivia. "He knows just the right thing to say and just when to say it. Even when he first came here. At first he said he had no inkling that Photon was anything more than a harmless pastime, and then he's saying that we're legends."

"Yeah, well . . . he was confused. Who wouldn't be?"

She looked at him. "*I* wouldn't be."

He shrugged and watched.

Baethan closed on Gambler and swung his staff. Had he connected, it would have cracked Gambler smartly on the head. Instead Gambler ducked under it and, with Baethan off balance, grabbed the staff and pulled it from the cyborg warrior's grasp.

Baethan stopped a moment and said, "The staff won't work for you, Gambler. Give it here."

Even as Baethan spoke, Gambler moved . . . backward. He backpedalled, brought the staff level and then charged forward. He slammed the end of the staff into the ground several feet in front of Baethan, kept on going and flew into the air. His feet slammed into Baethan's gleaming chest and the cyborg wizard stumbled backward. Then, leaping high in the air and spinning, Gambler delivered a reverse back kick to Baethan's moustached face.

Baethan's greatest weakness was his own weight, and once sent off balance it was only a matter of moments before he found himself flat on his back.

Gambler was on top of him, now holding the staff between his two hands and bracing the staff across Baethan's throat. He was grinning from ear to ear. "Give up, Baethan?"

"I yield," said Baethan. Gambler stepped off of him and Baethan hauled himself to his large feet.

"You're not mad, are you, Lord Baethan?"

"Certainly not," said Baethan. "I have no emotions. Anger is for lesser beings."

"Well, that's a relief. Besides, I was just lucky."

"This is true," intoned Baethan.

Bhodi snickered. Then suddenly MOM's voice sounded through Intellistar. "All Photon Warriors please come to the briefing room immediately."

Gambler looked up with excitement. "Sounds like I might be going on my first mission, huh, Baethan?"

"Lord Baethan," came the stiff reply.

"Sorry. Lord Baethan, are you sure you're not upset that I beat you?"

"Positive. I am incapable of irritation."

"Well, good. Because I—"

"Be quiet."

"Yes, sir."

Moments later they had assembled in the main room. Parcival and Pike came running in, and Parcival looked with astonishment at Bhodi Li. "Now, this is a first," he said. "You're always the last one here, Bhodi."

Bhodi shrugged expansively. "First time for everything, Parcival."

"Quiet, please," said MOM with uncommon harshness. "We have an emergency on our hands."

A dreary looking planet came onto the screen. "This," she said, "is planet M172—a bombed-out ruin of a planet. Captain Burnside from the planet Dekka was forced down by a ship from the Warlord of Arr. His last transmission to me was that he was bringing his ship into one of the fortresses left on the planet surface, but he wasn't able to tell me which one before his equipment failed."

Blinking dots were superimposed over three points on the planet. "There are fortresses at points north, east and west. They are not much more than burned-out structures, but it was a convenient landmark for Burnside to aim for."

"Is this Burnside particularly important?" asked Gambler.

Tivia turned to him, her eyes glaring. "Everyone is important," she said.

"But Captain Burnside is particularly important," said MOM. "He is carrying a cargo of pure Photonium. Even now the Dark Guardians are heading there in force to capture him and his cargo. Should the Dark Guardians obtain the Photonium, it would be a disaster of cosmic proportions."

"What are we standing around for?" said Bhodi. "Let's do it."

Gambler clapped Bhodi on the back. "We're going into it, partner. Wish me luck. But then"—he winked broadly—"Gamblers make their own luck. Don't they?"

5

Into the Fray

With steady hands, Leon guided the *Zephyr* to M172.

The ship went into orbit around M172, and Parcival checked the scanners. "No sign of any Arrian ship . . . but that doesn't necessarily mean anything."

Seated behind Parcival, Lord Baethan said sternly, "We must proceed with extreme caution. However, time is of the essence, so I recommend that we split into three groups. Myself and Tivia shall check the north fortress, Parcival and Pike shall take the east, and Bhodi and Gambler can take the west."

"I'll stay up here with *Zephyr* to watch for approaching Arrian ships. And if I see them first, then they'll see me last." Leon shook a fist fiercely.

Moments later each of the Photon Guardians had transported down in their respective teams. Leon turned to the lonely task of watching the monitors to make certain that no one crept up on them. It would be tremendously inconvenient, Leon thought, if he were blown up, because that would make the mission that much harder.

• • •

Bhodi felt a shiver down his spine as he looked upon what could be the future of his world if they weren't careful.

There was nothing but desolation, as far as the eye could see. A burned-out plain that had once contained cities, buildings, life—all gone now. All dead and dust.

And one other thing—the fortress. It loomed nearby, an erratically-shaped structure that had once been some sort of metal but now was covered with stone. Once it had been tall and gleaming, a structure that all those on the planet took pride in. Now the pride was gone, along with the people.

Bhodi felt a lump in his throat and then Gambler was next to him. "I bet we find the man, Dan."

Bhodi turned and looked at him curiously. "Why do you always do that?"

"Do what?"

"Talk in a rhyme."

"Oh, that. Just a slang."

"Oh." Bhodi pointed at the fortress. "Come on, let's see if that's where Burnside is."

They made their way towards the fortress. Huge rocks and boulders dotted the landscape, and they weaved their way through them. Bhodi had his phaser out, ready for trouble, but Gambler seemed completely at ease. His arms swung loosely at his sides. His boots, Bhodi couldn't help but notice, made no noise on the ground. He was easily the most silent stalker Bhodi had ever encountered.

Gambler was grinning. "My first mission. This is just incredible. This makes the game look just sick. I mean, how can you go back and play for points after you've been out here playing for real?"

"Practice," said Bhodi. "It never hurts to stay in prac—"

He stopped because Gambler was no longer listening. He had halted in his tracks, and his head was cocked slightly. His nostrils flared and his face became a mask of concentration. Then he turned to Bhodi and said, "Stay here. I'll be right back."

"Right back!" said Bhodi. "Wait a minute. I'm supposed to be keeping my eye on you. I can't let you just go wandering off."

"Look. It's all right, really. I just want to check something." He grinned. "Just trust me on this, okay? Swear to Kolker I'll be back in five minutes. Okay?" And before Bhodi could say anything further, Gambler had disappeared between the rocks.

Bhodi considered running after him, but Gambler seemed so urgent, and eager to please. Bhodi knew how he felt—when he had first joined the Photon Guardians, all he wanted to do was prove his worth. If giving Gambler five minutes on his own would help satisfy that need in the recruit, Bhodi could take the chance.

He holstered his phaser and leaned against one of the large rocks to await results. And exactly two minutes later the results came as a mocking voice said, "Well, well. Bhodi Li."

He spun, praying he wouldn't see what he knew he'd see.

His heart sank as he found himself surrounded on all sides by the six Dark Guardians.

Warriarr stepped forward, Mandarr to his right. Warriarr's four massive arms loomed before Bhodi as he said, "Ah, Bhodi Li. How nice of you to finally show up. It seems that we've been waiting ages for you. Isn't that right, Mandarr?"

"Simply ages," hissed Mandarr. He raised his phaser point-blank at Bhodi. "Let's kill him right now."

Warriarr put up one of his four hands as the other Dark Guardians came out from their shelter, all closing in, their weapons leveled: Destructarr with his massive arm cannon, Pirarr with his cutlass blaster, Bugarr with his gun and Dogarr with his weapon mounted on his huge, scorpionlike tail.

"We've been here for hours," continued Warriarr, in no hurry. "I'd have your precious MOM sent in for a checkup, if I were you. She was certainly slow off the mark this time. We've had more than enough time to check out the other two forts and confirm that this is where the shipment of Photonium crash-landed." He waved one massive arm in the direction of the fort. "We were about to launch our attack when we were fortunate enough to stumble upon you."

Through gritted teeth, barely able to contain himself, Mandarr snarled, "Warriarr, I'm in charge of this mission, and I say we kill him right now! He's been far too lucky in the past."

"Look," said Bhodi. "I could always come back when you guys have made your decision." He took a step back, but they all leveled their weapons at him and he froze.

"Do not remind me, Mandarr, that you are the leader," said Warriarr in a dangerous tone. "If I am currently out of favor with the Warlord, that is only temporary. Soon I shall be the favored Dark Guardian once again; so until that time, do not cross me, you reconstituted Earthling."

Dogarr snickered, which sounded like a wheezing freight train. He loved when Mandarr and Warriarr bickered.

Mandarr bristled and was about to reply when Warriarr continued, "However, you are probably correct. A dead Photon Warrior is one we no longer need concern ourselves about. You may do the honors, Mandarr."

Mandarr grinned and stepped forward, his gun never wavering from Bhodi's chest. "You should use projectons, as we do, boy. If you did, the worst that would happen is that you get sent back to your precious Intellistar if you're hit. As it is, well"—he sighed in mock sympathy even as his trigger finger started to tighten—"Bye-bye, Bhodi."

Bhodi crouched, prepared to leap upward, knowing that he would never be able to move faster than a phaser bolt.

A high-pitched whine filled the air, the sound of a

phaser blast, and Bhodi involuntarily flinched. Then he realized that it had not been he, but Mandarr, who had been hit.

Mandarr staggered, clutching at his chest plate, and he howled his hatred and fury. Then, in a pinwheeling shower of sparks, Mandarr vanished.

Bhodi leaped upward, out of the clutches of the confused Dark Guardians. Even as he arced skyward, another phaser blast cut from nowhere and nailed Warriarr squarely on his chest. With a shriek, Warriarr too discorporated, flashing back to Arr in failure.

Frantic now, the other Dark Guardians started firing randomly all about them. "We're surrounded!" shouted Bugarr. "Fire at will."

They could see absolutely no one. One moment they were fired upon from behind, the next phaser bolts were in front, then to the side. Bhodi, from hiding, watched in amazement as one by one each of the Dark Guardians was picked off. There were so many bursts of sparkling light as they vanished that it looked as if someone were setting off firecrackers.

It took only seconds. Almost as quickly as it had begun, the last of the Dark Guardians had been hit squarely in the chest plate and sent back to Arr. Their howls of fury seemed to echo for almost a minute after they were gone.

Bhodi waited to see what would happen. Had an armada of previously unknown Photon Warriors shown up and saved him? Had Tivia and Baethan or some of the others realized that Bhodi was in trouble and somehow managed to come to his rescue? But how was that possible, for they were separated by many miles of the planet's circumference.

That was when Gambler stepped out into the middl⌐ the rocky area where only moments before B⌐ thought he would be meeting his end. H⌐ and then straight at the place where B⌐ "You can come out now, Bhodi. They're

Slowly Bhodi came out from behind the rock. "You?" he asked incredulously. "You did all that?"

Gambler grinned. "Of course. Who else?"

"But—"

"Hey, no need to thank me." He tapped his nose. "Heightened senses. I smelled them coming. So I made myself scarce, waited until they showed themselves, and then started picking them off while I kept myself moving so they couldn't draw a bead on me."

Bhodi stood there, open-mouthed.

"Pretty slick, Nick. Huh?"

Bhodi closed his mouth and then said, "You could have at least told me what you had in mind. You just don't go running off like that. We're supposed to be a team."

Gambler looked at him in surprise. "No time. It all happened so fast. Besides, the whole thing about being a team is that you can trust each other. I wanted you to see that you could trust me. I said that I would handle it, and I did, didn't I? You've got to admit that."

"Yeah, well . . . I suppose so." He let himself grin. "Still, I would have been a little less nervous staring down Mandarr's gun if I'd known that a rescue was on the way."

Gambler clapped him on the shoulder. "Exactly! That might have tipped them off, and then they wouldn't have been such easy targets."

"All right, all right," Bhodi laughed, relief flooding over him at his near miss. "Next time, though, find some way to warn me. Okay?"

"Okay, Ray."

Ten minutes later they had made it to the fort, Bhodi in the lead, and they were just about to enter when a phaser bolt sliced over Bhodi's left shoulder. Bhodi and Gambler leaped back, guns drawn, and Bhodi shouted, "Who's in here?"

There was a silence, and then Bhodi called out, "We're

from the Photon Alliance. We've come to rescue you. MOM sent us.''

Another pause, and then a suspicious voice called out, ''How do I know you're with the Alliance? You could be one of the Warlord's creatures.''

Bhodi considered this for a moment and Gambler muttered, ''He's right. How do we prove we're the good guys?''

After another moment's thought, Bhodi called out, ''What do you call a ten-foot giant with a nine-foot sword?''

''What did you say?'' called out the voice in complete bafflement.

''I said, 'What do you call a ten-foot giant with a nine-foot sword?' ''

''I don't know,'' called the voice. ''What?''

Bhodi paused. ''Sir.''

Gambler groaned softly. Then they heard the voice call out again, ''Was that supposed to be funny?''

''Well, I thought so,'' replied Bhodi.

''What were you trying to prove?''

''Easy,'' called Bhodi. ''Can you imagine the Dark Guardians telling you jokes?''

Gambler stared at Bhodi in open disbelief. ''You've got to be kidding. You think that's going to convince h—''

The man stepped out into the open. He was now visible through the great door of the fort. ''You've got a point,'' he admitted.

Bhodi and Gambler exchanged looks, and Bhodi said smugly. ''Yeah, I think he'll fall for it.''

Bhodi stepped out, his phaser holstered, and walked slowly towards the bald, middle-aged man who awaited them. ''I'm Bhodi Li. This is Gambler.''

The man nodded. ''Captain Malcolm T.J. Burnside, at your service. You're just in time. I think the Warlord's men are somewhere in the vicinity.''

''They were,'' Gambler said, and aimed at an imaginary target with his phaser. ''Not anymore.''

"Well, I *am* impressed," said Burnside.

"So was I," said Bhodi. "Your cargo intact, captain?"

"Absolutely. The sealant held, which is fortunate. Pure Photonium is lethal."

"I know," said Bhodi, and for Gambler's benefit he said, "You have to convert Photonium to its crystal form in order for it to give light and life."

"Yes, crystal," said Burnside. "Much like this one."

He reached into the folds of his great black coat and pulled out a glowing round crystal. Gambler let out a low whistle. "So that's what those look like up close."

Burnside nodded. "Dekka is one of the major mining spots for Photonium and Photon crystals, and a major conversion center as well. This load of Photonium was discovered in one of our colony planets. It was a small deposit, relatively speaking. Cleaned out the entire she-bang, loaded it onto my ship and was transporting it to Dekka when the Warlord's men ambushed me. Lucky you folks came to bail me off of this lifeless hunk of rock."

Bhodi looked around and pursed his lips. "Yes, it is lifeless, isn't it?" Then he eyed the crystal.

Burnside caught on to what he was thinking and grinned. "Absolutely right. And I would be honored if this humble crystal could be utilized to restore some life to it."

He placed the crystal reverently down on the ground. It sparkled, inviting, a hub of infinite possibilities.

Bhodi said, "Gambler, would you care to do the honors? You've certainly earned it."

Gambler stared at the crystal, enraptured, and Bhodi saw with some surprise that the usual cocksure expression on his face was gone. "Uhm . . . you do it, Bhodi. I just . . . you do it, okay?"

Bhodi grinned, pleased that there was something in this world that was capable of catching the usually cocky Gambler off guard. If it took the beauty of a Photon crystal to do it, then so be it.

He raised his phaser and said, "The Light shines," and fired once.

The crystal lit up, flooded with every color in the spectrum. Light and warmth radiated out from it, suffusing the ground around it with green.

Grass, where there had been none before, began to push out from the ground. Rock softened to become dirt, ideal for life and growth. Beneath his feet Bhodi could sense small creatures coming into existence, creatures who would aid in the growth around them and eventually would evolve into whatever the indigenous life of this planet would be.

It spread outward, brushes and shrubs cracking through the surface, grabbing a tenuous and then stronger hold on life. Outward, ever outward went the magic of the Photon crystal, and M172 was in the light for the next one hundred years.

At the far northern fort, Tivia and Baethan were still exploring, looking for a hidden passage or some similar place where the pilot might have secreted himself. Tivia was leaning over a rock ledge when the rock under her suddenly transformed into dirt and crumbled under her. She fell only a couple of feet, just far enough to bruise her ego but nothing more.

As she brushed herself off, Baethan came up behind her, observing the green that was spreading around them. "It appears that someone in our group has alligned a crystal."

"So I noticed," commented Tivia. Her mask had slipped slightly and she adjusted it. As she did, Baethan had activated the communicator that was a part of his wrist assembly.

"*Zephyr*," he called. "This is Lord Baethan."

Leon's cheerful gravelly voice came right back. "Glad to hear from you, Baethan. I can imagine what you're calling about. From up here it looks like the entire planet has been brought into the Light. The origination of the wave was at the west fort."

Baethan and Tivia glanced at each other as Leon continued, "Looks like this one is Bhodi's game all the way."

Tivia nodded. "I don't know whether to be pleased that the mission is accomplished or concerned that Bhodi's going to become even more insufferable than ever."

"Do not worry," said Baethan matter-of-factly. "Perhaps it was Gambler who was responsible for the success of the mission."

"Thanks, Baethan," said Tivia with no enthusiasm. "You've just suggested the one thing that worries me more than Bhodi's ego growing: Gambler's ego growing."

As they walked out of the fort, Baethan said, "I do not comprehend your concern, Tivia. Frankly humanoid emotions are always something of a puzzle to me. Your apprehension seems based on no discernible data."

"I know. It's . . . a feeling. Haven't you ever had a feeling about something, Baethan?"

Baethan paused and considered. "Once I was being pursued by a dinosaur, and I had a feeling he would step on me. Is that of any help?"

Tivia laughed softly. "Not much, I'm afraid. But I appreciate the try."

Parcival looked up from the energy meters and nodded briskly at Burnside. "She's powered up. All ready to go."

Burnside confirmed Parcival's announcement from across the bridge, checking readings on his systems. "It was good of you people to charge up the power cells for me from your own ship's stores."

Parcival waved it off. "I also noticed a leak in your cells, probably from when you were hit by the Arrian ship. I've patched that up and they will last you on your trip to Dekka. After that, you better have new ones installed."

Burnside nodded. "I sure will. Be sure to relay my thanks to the rest of the Photon Warriors. I'm going to tell the Emperor about all the help you've been, and I'll bet you he invites you to one of his big bashes as thanks."

"That would be nice," said Parcival, but he sounded indifferent. Upon seeing Burnside's expression, he added hastily, "I'm afraid I've never been much for parties. But there are some in my group who will be extremely appreciative. Believe me."

"Okay," said Burnside, showing a toothy grin, "but be sure to have 'em keep a far distance from the Emperor's daughters. He's mighty touchy about them."

"I will," said Parcival, "should the occasion arise." He punched into the ship's subspace radio system. "Bring me up, Leon. I've got her all fixed up."

He stepped back, tossed a salute to Burnside, and then zipped upward in a burst of blue light.

Burnside shook his head, impressed. "They're really something, those people. Weirdest bunch I ever saw. But I'd sure rather have them with me than against me."

Moments later the crew of the *Zephyr*, still in orbit around the planet, watched as the cargo ship broke free of M172's gravity and, seconds later, leaped into hyperspace.

"That's that," said Leon. "Let's go home."

The *Zephyr* moved forward under Leon's steady hand, and as they leaped into hyperspace, coordinates set for Intellistar, something that one of the Dark Guardians had said percolated to the top of Bhodi's mind.

He leaned forward in his chair and said, "Hey, guys . . . why are we always risking our necks? Why don't we send out projectons the way the Dark Guardians do?"

They all turned and stared at him as if he'd suggested that they take a stroll in space with no suit.

"But . . . what fun would that be?" asked Leon.

"It's not a matter of fun," said Bhodi reasonably. "It just seems unfair that the Dark Guardians have this incredible advantage over us. Why hasn't MOM arranged for something similar for us, to even the odds a bit?"

"We're on the side of the Light, Bhodi Li," said Tivia. "That's all the advantage we need."

"Hey, a phaser bolt can't tell the difference between the good guys and the bad guys."

"Quite true," said Baethan. "But to attack your enemies in the manner that the Arrians do is the height of cowardice. We would not stoop to their level."

And it was Gambler who ended the discussion by saying, "Yeah, Bhodi. You have to be willing to take risks if you're going to have what it takes."

He grinned ingratiatingly and although Bhodi still wasn't certain that it made a lot of sense, he decided to let it slide. He imagined that if it were something that MOM had wanted them to do, she would have arranged for it ages ago. Everyone else had complete confidence in the super-computer, and he imagined that there was really no reason that he shouldn't either.

Still, he had a niggling feeling in the back of his mind that there was going to be big trouble ahead.

He kept his concerns to himself even after they had arrived at Intellistar. As he prepared for MOM to send him back to Earth, Gambler caught up with him in a corridor and said with an air of confidentiality, "That Tivia . . . I think she's warm for your form, Norm."

Bhodi stared at him. "Where have you been picking up Earth slang?"

"Listening to you and Parcival."

"Well, you know nothing about Tivia. She makes a very big deal over the fact that she doesn't need me and doesn't even like me."

Gambler draped an arm around Bhodi's shoulder and matched his stride. "Believe me"—his scarlet eyes glittered—"I know women. And the louder she says she doesn't like you, the more she does."

Bhodi eyed him. "Really?"

"Really." He grinned. "Believe me, I know women."

"Even women like Tivia?"

"Even them. Look, next time we get together, we'll sit

down and chat. I'll feed you some lines that'll have Tivia
eating out of your hand.''

Bhodi looked at his open hand. ''That's kind of tough to
believe. How can you be so sure of this?''

''What do you think?''

''I think that to talk like this, you must be really lucky
with girls.''

''Luck!'' Gambler laughed. ''It's like I always say . . .
Gamblers make their own luck.'' He spread his hands
wide. ''Hey. Trust me.''

And Bhodi would trust him. But it would turn out to be
one of the biggest mistakes in Bhodi Li's life.

6

B.Y.O.B. (Bring Your Own Blaster)

It was some weeks later, a beautiful Saturday morning, and Christopher Jarvis was indoors watching morning cartoons.

He was shaking his head in disbelief as his mother came by, and she watched over his shoulder as he popped another Cheez Doodle in his mouth. "What's the matter, Chris?" she asked.

He was leaning back in a recliner and now snapped it forward. "Can you believe this program?" he demanded, pointing to the animated antics on the screen.

"Probably not," she said reasonably. "I don't generally believe in cartoons. What program is it?"

"It's called *Laserblast University*," he said. "Get this. There's this girl from the thirtieth century who's a member of this university that keeps the peace, and she chases this bad guy back into our present day. The whole series is about this idiot trying to capture this one villain."

She tried to keep a straight face. "Sounds serious."

"Oh, it's just so stupid. I mean, here's the dumbest

part. In order to catch the guy, guess who she goes to for help?''

''The government?''

''Of course not. That would make sense. No, she teams up with her ancestors. Her ancestors, for heaven's sake! How could she be so dumb? If one of her ancestors gets killed, then she's endangering her own existence. Dumb dumb dumb.''

He shook his head, discouraged, and his mother ruffled his hair. ''Chris, this isn't high drama, for crying out loud. It's kid's television. Besides, she knows her ancestors won't get killed, because they have to be back for next week's episode.''

He sighed. ''Forget it, Mom.''

''Look, Christopher, you spend entirely too much time indoors anyway. You're either at school, indoors watching TV or else out playing Photon, which is also indoors. I know you get plenty of exercise, but you should be out in the sunlight, also. After all, honey, the light shines.''

He spun and stared at her. ''Why did you say that?''

''I don't know. It just occurred to me.''

At that moment the phone rang. He pounced on it before his mother could even fully register that it was ringing. At the same time his sister Kathy bolted out from another room, shouting ''It's for me!'' so quickly that it came out one word.

''Yo! Chris,'' Al's voice came over the phone.

Chris held up a hand and waved his sister off. ''Sorry, squirt. It's mine.''

Kathy made a little huffing noise and stomped off in irritation.

As Chris's mother walked away, shaking her head, he said. ''Hey, Al. What's cooking?''

''My folks are taking off for the weekend again. I'm going to shanghai the car again.'' Now Chris understood why Al was talking in such a low voice. ''I figured maybe you wanted to come along this time.''

"Look, Al, just because last time you managed to get away with it . . . I mean, luck was with you, but you can't count on that every time, you know?"

"Luck!" He sounded indignant. "We're not talking luck here, Chris. We're talking skill. So you in or out?"

At that moment Chris's ring started to flash. "Thanks, MOM," he said out loud.

From the kitchen his mother said, "You're welcome, dear. Thanks for what?"

"Oh, I wasn't talking to you, Mom, I was talking to . . . uhm, never mind." He spoke into the phone, "Thanks for the invitation, Al, but I've got something else cooking."

"What's her name, you sly dog?" Al chortled.

"Get your mind out of the gutter, Al," said Chris. "Can't talk now. See you later."

He hung up quickly, bounded to his feet, and barrelled out the door, past his startled mother who had not been anticipating such a blur of activity from her previously unmoving son.

As he pedalled furiously towards the Photon Center, his mind raced over the past several weeks of activity. Gambler had meshed with the rest of the team with incredible smoothness. He was easygoing, quick-witted, a superb fighter, fun to talk to. And so what if the first of the lines he had given Bhodi to try on Tivia had wound up with Bhodi getting his face slapped. Gambler had said that this was all part of the plan, and for all he knew, Gambler was right.

And yet . . .

There had been a number of occasions where they had been out in the field, and Gambler had taken some spectacular risk, some incredible chance. Once, Gambler had grabbed Tivia and made a death-defying swing on a vine over a huge chasm, in order to get away from a rampaging Owz that had been hot on their heels. The vine had snapped just as they reached the other side and they had landed with an undignified "whumpf." His daring in that instance had won over even Tivia, and yet . . .

And yet . . .

Chris thought about another time when he and Gambler had been off on their own, and just for target practice Gambler had taken a potshot at a baby Grontosaur. Unfortunately the mother Grontosaur had been in the vicinity, and Bhodi and Gambler had almost ended up as a late-afternoon snack.

Then there was the time that Gambler and Bhodi had gotten the drop on Mandarr. They could easily have zapped him back to Arr, but instead Gambler chose to holster his phaser and had leaped down to confront Mandarr one-on-one.

The fight had been brutal. Mandarr was a formidable hand-to-hand opponent and Gambler had almost gotten his head ripped off. Because Gambler was in the way, Bhodi had been unable to get a clear shot. As it turned out, Gambler had actually managed to beat Mandarr with a daring reverse snapkick that had brought the Dark Guardian to his knees. He had then put Mandarr out of his misery by shooting his chest plate.

"Gambler, that was just dumb," snapped Bhodi as Gambler dusted himself off.

"Hey, Bhodi, come on. We're at war with these freaks, not playing games with them," said Gambler, his expression still friendly. "A lot of war is psychological. By clobbering Mandarr man-to-man, we've got a whammy against him that we can use to our advantage next time."

"Either that or we just made him mad," said Bhodi.

"Hey, look, what's done is done. If you think I was out of line, then I'll watch it in the future. Just don't pass on your reservations, okay? If the others shared your opinion, I couldn't stand that. So keep it just between you and me, okay? Please?"

"I don't know . . ."

"Come on." He grinned. "Who's it going to hurt?"

Bhodi thought a moment, and then he said slowly, "On one condition."

"Anything, Bhodi. Anything."

Bhodi laughed. "Give me a line so that I won't get my face slapped again."

Now, as Chris biked towards the Photon Center, he ran that back through his mind and wondered if he hadn't made a mistake. All of the Photon Guardians were responsible for the training of their newest recruit, and his failure to report Gambler's excessively rash behavior might be viewed as a serious omission on his part.

Yet, he couldn't help but think of his own performance from time to time. The others were always chiding him that he was too rash, that he would go off on his own, that he would take unnecessary chances. Who was he to criticize? So what if Gambler was a little daring? That shouldn't be held against him. Maybe he, Bhodi, was becoming too much of a stick in the mud. Maybe he was even a little jealous.

Better to keep his peace for the time being. Better to stick with Gambler, who was the closest thing to a real friend he had among the Photon Guardians.

Why screw up a good thing?

Bhodi Li materialized in Intellistar, the last as usual.

"Someday," Tivia said, "you'll learn a lesson in punctuality, Bhodi."

Bhodi shook his head, holstering his phaser. "Frankly, I don't get it. Sometimes I think you people must be on roller skates, to get to your own Photon Centers as fast as you do."

Bhodi wasn't sure if Tivia was smiling under her mask, but her eyes crinkled just slightly. "Perhaps we are," she said. "Come on, Bhodi. We're getting an invitation."

He blinked even as he followed her. "Invitation? Where to?"

"What else? A party."

They went into the main conference room, where the other Photon Guardians were assembled. MOM's lights blinked a gentle welcome and she said, "Now that we are all here, it is my pleasure to tell you that I have gathered you together, not for a mission, but for once to celebrate a more festive occasion."

Tivia glanced at Bhodi. "See?"

"We have received an invitation from Emperor Flynn of the planet Dekka. You remember that some time ago you rescued one of his freighter captains from the Arrians. The Emperor would now like to hold a major celebration in your honor. I have taken the liberty of accepting for you—I did not think that any of you would object."

"No problems in this section," said Bhodi.

Gambler elbowed Bhodi playfully in the ribs. "This is our big chance. Flynn's parties are known throughout the cosmos. The best of everything, and I do mean everything."

"All riiiight."

Tivia sighed loudly. "Honestly, Bhodi, sometimes I'm concerned about the amount of influence you're having on Gambler."

"Oh, I'll try and be more careful in the future, Tivia," said Bhodi, and then he winked at Gambler.

"The party will commence upon your arrival," said MOM. "I must remind you that the Emperor is a valued and important member of the Photon Alliance. Dekka is a leading source and processor of pure Photonium. Emperor Flynn is sometimes a bit erratic, and I must ask you to treat him with the utmost deference and caution. Is that quite clear?"

They all nodded their understanding, and Bhodi couldn't help but notice that Gambler still had that wide grin on his face.

Minutes later the *Zephyr* launched from Intellistar towards Dekka.

"I'll lay in the coordinates for the hyperspace jump," said Parcival.

"Take your time, Parcival," rumbled Leon, staring through his viewscreen at the inviting darkness of space.

"I don't get out here near often enough. How about you, Lord Baethan?"

Baethan stared stonily ahead. "Outer space or planetside makes no difference to me," he said. "I see no intrinsic advantage of one over the other, with the possible exception of the fact that one does not need special equipment to survive on a hospitable planet. Outer space is inhospitable no matter where you go."

Bhodi slid over next to Tivia. She glanced at him and, looking away, said, "Remember what MOM said, Bhodi. Best behavior."

"Absolutely," said Bhodi. "Of course that applies to all of us."

She turned back and looked at him quizzically. "Now just what do you mean by that? Are you implying that I would in any way embarrass us?"

"Not at all," said Bhodi. "But I was wondering—for example, I understand the Emperor is something of a lady's man. How would you brush him off politely if he started putting moves on you?"

She seemed almost amused. "You mean would I slap his cheek?"

He flushed slightly. "Yeah. That's what I mean."

"I am impressed by your assumption, Bhodi, that I would necessarily want to."

He felt as if a hammer had hit him in the ribs. He glanced over and saw that Gambler was watching the conversation with extreme interest. Pike was busy expertly shuffling a deck of cards, which seemed to come alive in his accomplished fingers.

"Well, I just assumed," he said. "You've always said that you don't need any man . . ."

"A harmless humoring of an important member of the Alliance hardly constitutes a compromising of my principles," she said with one eyebrow arched. "Besides, Bhodi Li, if he is handsome or charming, it would be most flattering to have him exhibit interest in me. Even the women of my planet don't mind flattery now and then.''

"Really?"

"Yes, really."

He paused, searched for something to say. "You know, Tivia, you've got really great . . . uh . . . eyebrows."

She shoved him away and he heard a low, musical laugh issue from her mask. "Go strap in, Bhodi Li. When we jump into hyperspace, I'd hate to think of your incredibly flattering self being splattered all over the inside of *Zephyr*. If for no other reason than that MOM would probably ask me to clean you up."

"Now who's being flattering?" He stood up and crossed over to where Gambler was sitting. As Bhodi had taught him, Gambler raised a hand, palm upward, and Bhodi slapped him a high five, and Gambler then returned the salute.

"Looks like you two were getting friendly," said Gambler, his scarlet eyes sparkling with amusement. "And maybe you were getting lucky?"

Bhodi sat back, feeling smug. "Like you said yourself, Gambler, you make your own luck."

"True, true."

"Get ready, all of you," called Leon. "We're preparing to make the jump into hyperspace."

Space started to bend all around them, the stars running together in long white streaks. Bhodi remembered how impressed he was that the jump into hyperspace in real life so strongly resembled the hyperspace jump in *Star Wars*, although Leon never understood why Bhodi occasionally called him "Han."

"Here we go," called Leon, and with the engines roaring they made the full jump into hyperspace.

Space turned completely inside out as they cut sideways into the faster-than-light realm of hyperspace . . . and that was when all hell broke loose.

There, framed against the turbulence of hyperspace,

were three ships belonging to the Warlord of Arr. They were not moving. Instead they were waiting for the *Zephyr* with great patience.

Leon saw them first and madly swerved to port. The Photon Warriors were thrown against their chairs and Parcival shouted, "Leon, what are you doing?"

"Dark Destroyers," was the terse reply. "Three of them."

"That's impossible!" said Parcival. "They can't have been waiting for us. You can't just float in hyperspace! You have to keep moving or you drop back to sublight speeds."

"I had astrophysics for breakfast decades before you were born, Parcival! Don't lecture me!" snapped Leon. He veered the ship again and glanced in his rear monitor. "Blast! They're right on us."

Ray blasts flashed to the left and right of the ship, and Leon quickly snapped the shields up. Just in time, for the entire ship shook as several blasts hit home on their rear engines' shields. They were protected, but only as long as the shields held out.

Parcival madly tried to run calculations through his computer. "Leon, we're lost," he wailed. "I have nothing to recalibrate from."

Bhodi unbuckled and lurched forward to Parcival's side. "Let's just get out of here!" he snapped.

"Don't you think I want to?" demanded Parcival. "But we have to recalibrate or we could come out of hyperspace practically anywhere. In the middle of an asteroid belt, in the center of a sun—anywhere!"

"That's just great."

"Cloak us, Leon," snapped Baethan.

"Not a good idea," Leon replied, angling the ship sharply away from the Dark Destroyers. "There are too many of them. Cloaking will take too much power from the shields, and if they fire randomly, they have a pretty good shot of hitting us even if we're cloaked. We've got to fight."

And with that he arched the ship around and shot straight back at the Dark Destroyers.

Tivia choked back a scream. "Leon, are you crazy!?"

"You have a better idea?" replied Leon.

Gambler had unstrapped as well, and he was at Leon's side, staring out the viewing port. His eyes narrowed, he seemed to be reaching out. Suddenly he pointed. "There—810-mark-3. Correct course, now!"

"What?"

And now Baethan was next to them as well. "He's right. It's our best chance. Change course and head there full speed."

"Leon!" shrieked Tivia. "The Destroyers!"

They loomed in front of the *Zephyr*, cutting loose with full armament. The ship lurched and a blinking light came on.

"Shield overload," grated Leon. "Now or never. Parcival! Those coordinates Gambler said."

"Locked in," said Parcival. "Do it!"

Barely a hundred kilometers away, with space a bizarre joke all around them, the *Zephyr* suddenly dropped down and away like a stone from the Arrian ships. The Arrians immediately went into pursuit as the *Zephyr* screamed towards the spot Gambler and Baethan had agreed upon.

"I don't see anything special ahead!" shouted Bhodi, and then abruptly he felt like his entire body had imploded.

Somewhere distant he heard screams from Parcival, Gambler and Tivia, and a low moan from Pike. Everything had gone completely black. He felt his blood freeze, his skin ice over, and he knew with bleak certainty that if they didn't get out of wherever they were, he was going to die here, now, in the black emptiness of space, and no one on Earth would ever know what happened to him, and . . .

There was a sudden lurch and Bhodi felt his stomach drop from his throat back to its more customary location in his body. He looked around, blinked and to his astonishment saw that the stars were now normal.

"Wh—what happened?" he asked shakily.

Gambler turned, his usual jovial expression gone. He was all business now. "We powerdove into a black hole. Black holes are natural portals between hyperspace and normal space. Only problem is, it's dangerous as all get out. Of course," he added reasonably, "so is being blasted to free-floating atoms by an Arrian spacecruiser."

"Where are we, anyway?" asked Pike. "How far are we off course?"

Parcival punched up a star map on the navigational computer. "Let me check. Okay, we're . . ." He choked off in astonishment. "Extraordinary!"

"What? Give already, Parcival. What is it?"

"We're practically a stone's throw from Dekka," he said incredulously. "Now that's luck."

Bhodi turned towards Gambler. "Don't say it."

"Hey, not word one do you hear from me, McGee," said Gambler, letting out a long breath. "There's luck and then there's luck." He leaned over. "Hey, Parcival . . . what's that blinking light mean?"

Parcival looked where Gambler was pointing, and moaned. "It means we're in trouble again. Leon!"

Leon snapped on the rear monitor and there were the three Dark Destroyers hot on their tail.

Ahead of them loomed the planet Dekka, and right behind them, gaining speed, were the Destoyers.

"Tivia! Man the rear cannons!" called Leon.

Even as Tivia moved down a corridor to the station, she could be heard to mutter, "You could pick a better expression than 'Man the cannons,' you know."

A call came over the subspace radio. "Dekka Control to incoming ships. Veer off. You are approaching the planetwide shield. Contact at your speeds would mean instant destruction."

Tivia leaped into the rear cannon station, snapped the

gun into active mode and turned on the tracker. The three ships instantly came on, and her fingers flew, trying to bring the targeter to bear on one of the ships.

"This is *Zephyr*," Parcival said into the radio, trying to keep as calm as possible. "We've been invited, but it seems we have some unwanted pursuers on us."

"Understood, *Zephyr*. Maintain exact course, repeat, maintain exact course. Deviation could result in unpleasant accidents. Understood?"

"Understood."

The ship lurched under a direct hit from a Destroyer. Leon fought to bring the ship back on track and Tivia mouthed a silent curse, for the impact had knocked a target right out of her sight. Tivia readjusted, and slowly brought one of the fast-moving ships directly into her electronic cross hairs.

"The Light shines," she muttered, and punched the trigger.

The phaser cannon cut loose, strafing one of the Dark Destroyers, hammering away. It ate through the Destroyer's shields as if they were cotton candy, and pounded through to the guts of the ship.

One of the three pursuing ships now exploded. Under her mask Tivia smiled grimly.

Through the dust and debris that was all that remained of the destroyed ship, the remaining two Arrian ships pursued their target.

They concentrated their fire on *Zephyr's* rear deflector and, seconds later, cut through. The cannon station short-circuited and exploded, and Tivia now found herself trapped under collapsing metal.

The hull had been massively dented inward, and her mind screamed to her, They're going to breach the hull. They'll breach the hull and I'll be sucked out into space, into airless, dark space—

"*Bhodi!*" she screamed. "*Help me!*"

Bhodi, thirty yards away in the bridge, heard her and immediately ran to her. Gambler pounded after him.

Parcival glanced back, then looked at his computations. "Leon, we've lost our rear deflectors," he reported, his voice deliberately controlled. "Fifteen seconds to Dekka. Can you hold them off?"

"Don't see much choice, do you? Hold on!"

The *Zephyr* swung from side to side. Space seemed to explode around them from all the near misses of the two Destroyers.

Bhodi lurched from one side of the narrow corridor to the other. Then he saw Tivia, pinned in the seat in the compartment that housed the rear cannon. There was desperation in her eyes as she tried to shove at the metal that had her trapped, but she was off balance and couldn't apply the leverage.

Without hesitation Bhodi reached in and, applying his full strength, he hauled the metal off her. He started to help her climb out of the compartment—

A direct blast ripped open the compartment beneath Tivia's feet. With a shriek Tivia fell into space.

7
Planetfall

Almost.

"Tivia!" shouted Bhodi, and heedless of his own safety he grabbed her by the forearm. Her fingers desperately wrapped around his elbow and for a long moment they froze there like that, Tivia dangling into space and Bhodi her only lifeline.

There was no banter now, no snide remarks or jests. There was only fighting for life. Bhodi, fighting the pull of space himself, braced with one foot and started to draw Tivia back into the ship. But the pull was overwhelming and for one instant Bhodi himself was about to be sucked out into space as well.

And then Gambler was there. He came up behind Bhodi and snared a rope around Bhodi's waist, then darted back and looped the other end around a huge overhead pipe that snaked its way through the ship. Then he just held on for dear life, pulling as hard as he could.

Bhodi strained every muscle in his powerful arms and slowly he started to haul Tivia, inch by inch, back into the ship. The mesh of her armor protected her from the ravages of space, but if he didn't get her in within seconds, she would asphyxiate. Now there was a horrible thought—Tivia dying right in front of him, and his being unable to do anything.

It was only then that he realized his own lungs were screaming for oxygen, and he had no time to be delicate. Bracing himself, breathing a prayer, Bhodi Li pulled with all his strength.

Tivia flew into the ship like a cork popped from a bottle. She landed on top of Bhodi and wrapped herself around him, her eyes closed against the terror of her near death. But the vacuum was not through with them, and they both started to slide across the deck, air rushing through the hole.

Then there was a flash of light past them, and a block of solid Photon light materialized over the hole. Bhodi sucked air deeply into his tortured lungs and Tivia, on top of him, did the same.

Behind them Lord Baethan was there with his staff, completing the patchwork job. It wasn't fantastic, but it was enough to serve for the present.

On the bridge, Parcival shouted, "Five seconds to Dekka!"

"We're going to hit the shield!" called Leon. "It's been a pleasure working with you, Parcival."

Directly before them was the greenness of Dekka, and between them and Dekka was an absolutely impenetrable force field, the only protection that Dekka had ever needed. And the Photon Guardians were about to wind up as a splotch against it.

Suddenly, directly in front of them, a hole opened.

Since the force shield was invisible, naturally they couldn't see the hole either. But Parcival's instruments told him of its existence a split instant before they actually darted through it. Even as he said, "Leon, there's a gap!" they were through.

The Arrian ships detected the hole as well, and they powerdove towards the breach in Dekka's defense. The lead Destroyer was meters away when the hole resealed itself.

The lead Destroyer crashed into the shield. The nose of the ship was halted immediately, but due to the laws of physics the rear of the ship kept right on going. In the blink of an eye the Arrian Destroyer was about as threatening as a pancake, and about as flat, too.

Realizing at the last moment, the remaining Arrian ship veered upwards. The underside scraped against the shield and the Destroyer bounced slightly as it angled away in frustration from its prey.

"We're clear!" called Leon. "I can't believe it, but we're through."

"It was only logical," said Parcival, but inwardly he breathed a sigh of relief. He glanced over at Pike, calling, "Are you okay, Uncle Pike?"

Pike, over in his chair, was snoring peacefully.

Parcival whistled. "Talk about your confidence," he muttered. Then he went back to his instruments to navigate Leon to a safe landing.

Over by the phaser cannon, Bhodi and Tivia were still gasping for breath. Gambler was slumped against the wall inspecting woefully the torn skin on his hand where he had been pulling on the rope. Baethan was concentrating on maintaining the patch until they were planetside.

Tivia looked down at Bhodi. "You . . . you weren't going to let go. You could have been pulled to your death as well, but you weren't going to let me go."

A dozen flip answers leaped to his mind, but he dismissed them all as he spoke the simple truth. "Of course not."

Tivia reached to the bridge of her nose and pulled down the mask that covered the lower half of her face. She wrapped her arms around Bhodi's head and kissed him full on the mouth.

Bhodi felt as if his entire body had been jump-started. He reached around to embrace her and then, as quickly as it had happened, it was over. Tivia stood, wavering slightly on unsteady legs, and pulled the mask back over her face.

"Thank you," she said formally, and then she walked away.

Bhodi was left lying there, trying to commit the taste of her lips to memory before it disappeared completely. He heard a low laugh behind him and turned. Gambler was grinning ear to ear. "Bhodi, my friend, when you decide to impress a girl, you just go all out, don't you?"

"You saw it. I didn't imagine it, then. I mean, she's kissed me before, on the cheek. You know, like friends. But—"

"That wasn't any 'like friends' that I ever saw," crowed Gambler. "You got her, man. She's hooked. All you have to do is play it cool now. Sooner or later, she's yours. Am I right, Lord Baethan?"

"The frolics of humans are of no interest to me," said Baethan distractedly.

Gambler nodded as if Baethan had just backed him up. "There you have it. You know I'm right, Dwight."

He hauled Bhodi to his feet and they high-fived each other. Baethan "harrumphed" deep in his bio-mechanical throat.

"Report," rumbled the Warlord over the viewscreen.

The Soldarr, on the bridge of the remaining Dark Destroyer, faced his lord and master with trepidation. The rest of the crew stood nearby, eager to see what would happen.

"We were awaiting them in hyperspace as planned, my Lord," said the Soldarr.

"And you are contacting me to inform me that they have been destroyed?" His dark image seemed to grow larger on the screen.

"Well," said the Soldarr, "actually, no, my Lord.

They managed to elude us in hyperspace and escape through a black hole. But we pursued them, only they blew one of us up and then got through the Dekkan shield before we could destroy them. Our second ship was demolished against the shield.''

"So what you are saying," said the Warlord of Arr in careful, measured tones, "is that you are the last surviving ship.''

"That is correct, my Lord."

There was a long silence and then the Soldarr said, "My Lord. Do you have any instructions for me?"

"Three battle cruisers, and you could not destroy one ship of Photon Guardians." He was shaking his dark and shapeless head. "A pity. No, Soldarr, I have no further instructions for you.''

"But, my Lord," said the Soldarr, "What should I— Arrrrgggghh!''

Dark flame erupted from within the Soldarr, blossoming forth from the folds of his cape and mask. Within seconds it had completely enveloped him. The other Soldarrs dropped back in horror and fear as the commander burned to death before their eyes.

When the screeching stopped, and when there was nothing but a pile of ashes on the floor, the image of the Warlord spoke to no one Soldarr in particular.

"We know where the Photon Guardians are," he said. "They can't stay there forever. Therefore, stay in orbit about the planet. I will dispatch the Dark Guardians in two ships, and they are to be given full charge of this mission. If, before the Dark Guardians arrive, the Photon Warriors attempt to leave Dekka, you are to utterly destroy them. Otherwise, you will not be returning to Scarrcastle.''

The Warlord blinked off, and although the Soldarrs would not voice any such sentiment, they all felt the same thing. Somehow, not returning to Scarrcastle did not sound like the worst idea of the day.

• • •

The *Zephyr* plummeted downward.

Bhodi and Gambler ran to the front, where the rest of the crew except for Baethan had already taken up stations.

"How are we going to land this thing?" demanded Bhodi. "I don't exactly see any landing gear."

"That's because you're assuming that the *Zephyr* is like any other ship," said Parcival. "But it's not. It's bio-mechanical, just like Intellistar." He reached over and flipped open a panel. Inside the panel was a set of dials, and with quiet expertise Parcival began to manipulate them.

The exterior of *Zephyr* began to glow. The large fin on her underside appeared to melt upward into the ship's belly, leaving an absolutely smooth underside.

Leon, in the meantime, fired the retrojets and broke the ship's forward motion. Bhodi braced himself but Gambler tumbled forward, as did Tivia. Pike snored louder.

The ship leveled out, the atmosphere screaming around them. The exterior of the ship began to heat up but inside there was no discomfort at all.

"There," said Leon.

In front of them lay the Dekkan spaceport. There were a number of ships already clustered about and Leon aimed for a deserted area.

A voice crackled over the radio. "*Zephyr,* you are cleared for landing. Sorry about the trouble with the Arrian ships."

Leon snorted. "Not half as sorry as the Arrians are."

The ship circled the spaceport in one leisurely turn, then Leon brought her about until he was just above the spot he wanted to be, except about five thousand feet too high.

It was hard to believe that Leon's massive hands were capable of such precise movements, but they were. He effortlessly brought *Zephyr* down in a perfect vertical landing into the spaceport.

The moment they settled onto the ground, all the Photon Guardians, with the exception of Baethan (who had now come forward and allowed the temporary seal to disappear) let out a collective sigh of relief.

And then, from outside, there was the huge roar of a crowd. The Photon Guardians stared at each other, not having the faintest idea what the whole brouhaha was about.

"Do you think they're under attack?" asked Bhodi.

"Well, if they are," said Leon, patting his shoulder cannon, "Leon's ready."

"Before we plunge headlong into danger, it would be advisable to check the exterior monitors," said Baethan evenly.

Parcival's hands were already moving across the control. "Way ahead of you, Baethan."

An image snapped up on the viewing screen. There was a mob outside, some fifty meters from the ship, and they were waving their arms and shouting. Instinctively Bhodi reached for his phaser, certain that angry crowds were waiting for them.

Then Parcival brought up the audio and over it filtered cheers of "Photon Warriors, way to go!" and "Hurray for the Photon Guardians," and, perhaps the most gratifying, "The Light shines!"

Parcival half smiled. "They sound deadly, Bhodi. You'd better go first. We'll cover you as best we can."

Bhodi laughed and holstered his phaser. As Parcival opened the exit hatch, Bhodi and Gambler, of one mind, gestured broadly for Tivia to take the lead. "After you," said Bhodi.

From her backpack, Tivia had pulled her long white mantle. As she draped it over her shoulders, Bhodi said, "That's your invisibility cloak. Are you expecting trouble?"

"Not particularly," she said. "It just makes me look good."

Immediately the response, "Particularly when you use it to disappear," leaped to Bhodi's mind, but he bit off the snide answer before he even began to say it. Instead he said simply, "You're right. It's real stylish."

He could tell she was smiling under her mask. "Why, thank you, Bhodi." She swirled the cape around her and walked out.

Without saying a word, Gambler high-fived Bhodi.

Over in his chair, Pike came awake with a yawn. "Are we there yet?"

Parcival chucked Pike affectionately on the shoulder. "Yes, Pike, we're here."

"Oh good. I knew we'd get out of trouble."

Parcival laughed. "You must have been confident to have gone to sleep during it."

Pike stretched. "Late-night card game," he yawned. "Have to rest up wherever I can. Besides, there wasn't anything I could have done except be nervous, and what good would that have done anyone?"

"Right as always, Pike."

They stepped out onto the gangway, the seven Photon Warriors, and they waved at the crowd. Gambler, out of the corner of his mouth, said, "I could really get into this."

"I know what you mean," said Bhodi.

The air was crisp but not cold. Far in the distance, as far as the eye could see, were mountain ranges. It was from these mountains that the Photonium was mined. Off to the left they saw a great wall, as high as an office building, and visible just over the wall were the tops of ornate towers.

"What's that?" he asked.

They started down the gangplank towards the cheering crowds. As a representative of the Dekkan Emperor rolled towards them, arms outstretched in greeting, Leon was saying, "That's the great wall of the capital city. Before the Dekkans discovered their unbreakable force field, back when they still fought land wars with each other, they created massive protective walls around their cities. Makes them darn near impregnable.''

"So there's no war on Dekka?"

"That's right," said Leon. "Sounds boring, doesn't it?"

The emissary greeted them broadly. He was of the species known as a High Roller. He was six and a half feet tall, his body long and angular. The lower third of his body was one solid mass, and on either side were large green organic wheels that propelled him forward, with a third, smaller wheel in back for additional balance. His face appeared completely blank, but upon closer inspection Bhodi could see a dozen little eyes, somewhat like a potato. His arms were long and thin, and they bent at three evenly spaced points rather than simply at an elbow.

He bowed slightly. "Greetings, all-mighty and wonderful Photon Warriors. I am Catron, emissary from Emperor Flynn. It is a pleasure to meet such renowned and great warriors.''

Bhodi extended a hand. "Glad to be here.''

Catron tilted his head a moment, then took Bhodi's hand and shook it briskly. When he released it, Bhodi found a trace of some sort of substance on his hand. He wiped it off on his armor and made a mental note not to shake hands with the green-skinned alien again.

Catron waved expansively. "Welcome to Dekka, capital city of the planet Dekka.''

"Easy to remember," observed Bhodi.

If Catron had a mouth, he would have smiled. Instead he inclined his head and said, "I'm glad that you are pleased. The hospitality of the planet Dekka is open to all of you. Everyone here is your deepest and most eternal friend.''

Before he could continue, a huge, hulking warrior leaped to the forefront of the crowd. He aimed a massive blaster.

Runya, the loser who felt himself cheated, now knew revenge to be his. "Die, Pike!" he bellowed, and fired.

8

Royal Pain

In that moment, as time seemed to lengthen interminably, a question abruptly posed itself to Bhodi Li. How was it that Catron had been able to speak to them, when he had no visible mouth? Where was his voice coming from?

It was at that moment, as his mind asked the question, that he received his answer.

Even as Runya was shouting and firing, Catron was moving. To be specific, Catron had been moving before Runya had begun to shout, and as Runya fired, Catron had covered the distance between himself and Runya with blinding speed. His arm, long and malleable, lashed out and snared around Runya's wrist. He yanked Runya's arm upward and the blast from the gun passed harmlessly over Pike's head.

So quickly had all this occurred that even before the quickdraw Bhodi Li had cleared his holster, Catron had already subdued the infuriated alien.

"You know the rules," Catron's voice sounded in his

head, and Bhodi realized that that was where he had been hearing the voice all along.

"A telepath," breathed Parcival.

Catron turned his blank face towards them. "Of course," he thought at them, and Bhodi now saw that the sides of his head pulsed slightly whenever he communicated. "No matter what sentient being the Emperor might encounter, having an emissary who can communicate with anyone is an absolute necessity."

Runya tried to pull his arms away to get off another shot at Pike. "Let go of me, you two-wheeled freak."

"Three-wheeled," thought Catron politely, and with a strength that one would never have suspected in those stalklike arms, he pulled the gun out of Runya's hand and tossed it to the Photon Guardians disdainfully. Bhodi caught it and stuck it in his belt.

"Pike!" howled Runya. "We have a score to settle."

"Not as far as I'm concerned," said Pike mildly. "You shouldn't be a poor sport, Runya. Besides, we're guests of this planet. You're worse than a poor sport. You're impolite."

Runya snarled, but Catron was unflappable. "Runya," he thought, and there was a dangerous undercurrent to his thought transmission, "as Pike says, he and his companions are guests of the Emperor, and are to be treated with the highest respect. Even by visitors to Dekka such as yourself."

"I warned you!" howled Runya, and he grabbed forward as if to strangle Catron. Bhodi took a step forward and then halted.

Catron was spinning his wheels backward at high speed. From a standing start he went from zero to sixty in under five seconds. He was still holding Runya's arm, and he dragged the furious four-armed alien behind him.

Across the landing area they went. The crowd howled as Catron shot across the strip as if jet-propelled. Runya was helplessly flailing his arms and legs, trying to find an anchor and failing.

As he towed his unwilling passenger, Catron thought at him in a deceptively friendly fashion.

"There is no fighting on Dekka, my dear Runya," he thought. "We are a peace-loving people. We have no intention of winding up as did our ancestors' neighbors on planet M172—a bombed-out wasteland. The only fighting permitted is trial by combat, and only then for someone who has broken the laws of the planet. Do you understand what I'm saying to you?"

"Let me go!" screeched Runya. Actually it wasn't quite that simple, for since he was being dragged around, it actually took him much longer to say, and there was quite a bit of voice catching in between the elongated syllables.

"Now Pike has just gotten here," thought Catron as if Runya had not even spoken. "It seems unlikely that he has broken any laws during the thirty seconds that he's been on our planet. You, on the other hand, pulled a weapon and threatened a guest of the Emperor. Now, that's breaking the law. If Pike chooses to press the matter, you could find yourself in serious trouble."

Because it was a thought broadcast, Pike, as did everyone else, heard the running commentary as clear as a bell. Unsure of how to project his own thoughts, Pike said out loud, "Oh, that's really not necessary. I have no intention of pressing any charges."

"Now, that's very fortunate for you, Runya. You should be sure to thank Pike, when next you see him."

He released the alien then and wheeled back across the landing pad. Politely he thought, "I apologize for this mishap, guests of the Emperor. Had I not been so excited by your presence, I assure you that I would have picked up on his hostile thoughts before he could have posed a threat to you."

Pike, as the offended party, could only say, "Oh, that's all right."

"Come," gestured Catron. "There is much to do. The Emperor would like to meet you as soon as possible."

Just before they were swallowed by the crowd, Bhodi glanced back at the massive Runya, who had just managed to pull himself to his feet. Even from this great a distance he could sense the fury and hatred that radiated from this savage creature, and he couldn't help but wonder what horrendous affront Pike had committed that could have caused this creature to seek his destruction.

"A card game?"

Bhodi was staring at Parcival in disbelief as the youngest Photon Warrior laced up the sandals that were part of the ceremonial clothes the Emperor had requested they wear.

Indeed, the Emperor's requests, made through his various representatives, had strained the patience of the Photon Guardians to the limit. Their weapons had been safely stored after repeated assurances from the Emperor's people that the detection devices outside the palace would pick up any weapons that anyone attempted to smuggle in. Furthermore, there were traditional garments that looked largely like kaftans that he had requested they wear. Bhodi had grumbled loudly that they were going to look as if they'd just stepped out of a Turkish sauna, but the reluctant consensus of the Guardians was that they should try and humor the Emperor whenever and wherever possible.

"Pike says it's a matter of great pride to Runya," said Parcival, finishing one sandal and starting on the other.

Nearby, Gambler luxuriated in a large sunken bathtub. Bhodi and Parcival had already availed themselves of the bathing facilities, and now it was Gambler's turn to enjoy the good life. His dark blue hair glistened and hung close over his face.

"I can understand Runya's point of view," said Gambler. "A card game is pretty darned important, if you ask me."

Bhodi wrestled with the complicated belts to close the elaborate costume, as he had no desire to have the stupid garment come open in the middle of the court. He looked around again at the alien architecture and marveled at it. Large curved couches and chairs were set into huge arches that stretched from floor to ceiling. He shook his head. "It's like the whole place was designed by Ronald McDonald."

"Who?" asked Gambler.

"Some clown," said Parcival.

"Oh." Gambler worked up a lather with the soap that floated nearby.

Leon walked out of a side room, the long garment swishing around his legs. They had had to search long and hard to find a garment large enough to fit the massive Leon. He stretched and said, "That hydrosonic shower is the best thing I've had in years. Really makes my scales tingle. Pike's finishing up now. Lord Baethan, you ought to try it."

Baethan was hunched over a viewing screen, studying the history of Dekka. He shook his head distractedly. "I am cyborg. I am not in need of the usual amenities afforded to creatures such as yourselves."

Bhodi suddenly remembered the tin woodsman from *The Wizard of Oz* being polished up by a giant buffer before seeing the Wizard. He pictured Baethan flat on his stomach, singing cheerfully, and started to laugh uncontrollably.

Parcival looked up. "What's the matter with you?" he asked.

Bhodi leaned down and whispered in his ear. Parcival looked over at Baethan and started to snicker, then laugh with uncontrolled hilarity. Baethan, glancing their way, was fully aware that somehow he had provided them with a source of tremendous amusement. He did not know why, nor did he particularly care. It was just another one of the minor indignities about which he had resigned himself upon deciding to associate with humans and other lesser life forms.

Tivia strode in, calling, "When are you six going to be finished in here?"

Gambler let out a squeal and dove beneath the waters of the bath. Bhodi, upon seeing Tivia, let out an appreciative whistle. Her kaftan was similar to theirs, but was slit up the side almost to her hip, displaying a generous amount of very shapely leg.

She put up a warning finger. "One word out of you, Bhodi Li, just one word, and I'll use you for nunchuk practice."

He put up his hands. "I won't say a word. But can I think a few?"

"I don't know. Can you?" She sighed. "If MOM hadn't asked for our tolerance . . . Gentlemen, the Emperor has requested our presence within the next five minutes. Let's try not to disappoint him, because if we do, he might come up with even more ludicrous outfits for us to wear."

She turned and walked out. Bhodi watched her go in silent admiration. Then he reached over and, sticking his hand into the bath, grabbed a fistful of Gambler's hair and pulled him to the surface. "Hey," he said, "Tivia says front and center in five minutes or she's coming in there after you."

Gambler's scarlet eyes seemed to consider that. "You know, that's probably the best offer I've had all day. Possibly all y—glub!" and he snorted water as Bhodi shoved his head back under.

The Emperor's throne room was much like the dressing room they'd been in earlier. High arches, gleaming, and the floor beneath them made from a shiny material that Bhodi didn't recognize. It suffused the room with a gentle white light.

"Not too shabby," muttered Gambler under his breath.

Bhodi was assessing the other beings in the court. There

was a wide assortment of aliens, including, Bhodi realized, himself. There were a couple of Lizoids with whom Leon was trading stories. And even another Celtar cyborg wizard who was engaged in deep conversation with Baethan.

Tivia drew close to him. "I feel ridiculous in this costume," she muttered.

"But you look spectacular. Look, it's not like you have to wear a chicken head or something. The only thing this outfit is doing is showing off your legs, which is what is really bothering you."

"That's right," said Tivia crossly. "I fight to make certain I'm respected as a warrior and an equal, and then I'm thrust into this position where I'm going to be accorded the same respect generally given to a piece of meat."

"You mean," asked Bhodi, "you're annoyed because you're concerned over how this is going to affect my opinion of you? Does what I think carry that much weight with you?"

She stared at him over her mask, and at that moment Catron rolled into the middle of the throne room. "All sentient beings," he thought out. "Please take your places. Emperor Flynn is on his way."

He rolled over to the Photon Warriors and indicated a section where they should sit. They did so, although Leon and Baethan found it difficult to maneuver into seats so low-slung and elected instead, for dignity's sake, to stand.

There was a fanfare from an invisible speaker, and Emperor Flynn entered the throne room.

He was remarkably humanoid—remarkably because, as far as Bhodi was concerned, after seeing such an array of creatures this day, he was expecting the Emperor to be something really bizarre. Such, however, was not the case. The Emperor looked like a man in his late forties, early fifties. He walked slightly stoop-shouldered. His gray hair was extremely thin on top and his sideburns came down to the line of his angular cheeks. What was obviously different about him were his eyes. They were huge, each one taking up almost the entire upper half of his face. And they were wide and sad looking, like a beagle who had just been tossed out of his umpteenth car.

His robes, similar to everyone else's, except a deep lavender, swirled around his feet like a miniature dust storm. He turned and sat heavily on his throne, then looked around at the inhabitants of his court.

He stared at them for a full moment, unmoving, not even breathing visibly. At length Gambler leaned over and whispered in Bhodi's ear, "Look, maybe I'm out of line here, but . . . is he alive?"

"I think so," Bhodi muttered back.

At that moment, as if stuck with a cattle prod, the Emperor leaped to his feet, a grin splitting his face. "That's right!" he cried, as if he'd just hit on the solution to universal peace. "Now I remember what we're doing today! We're having a party for the Photon Guardians." He leaned off the edge of the throne. "Now, just where are those crazy guys and gal?"

Baethan took a step forward, his metal foot clanking heavily on the polished floor. "We are the Photon Guardians," he said.

"Fantastic!" exclaimed the Emperor. All his previous lethargy seemed to have completely vanished. "Now, I know all the names, but I'll be blasted into space dust if I can remember which is which. Why don't you all introduce yourselves around?"

Each of the Warriors politely did so, giving name and planet of origin, and each was greeted with respectful applause. Those who had other natives from their homes in attendance got louder applause. Except for the other cyborg wizard, of course, who considered it far too undignified to applaud for Baethan.

Once they had introduced themselves, the Emperor stood and stretched out a hand. Silence immediately fell on the group. Silence, although not a Hush, for none had been invited.

"These Photon Guardians," intoned the Emperor, "saved the life of Freighter Pilot Captain Burnside, and an entire shipment of Photonium from the clutches of the Arrian empire. Furthermore, through the beauty of their Photon power, they have chosen to bring new life to planet M172."

There was a gasp of awe that sustained itself until the Emperor made a quick cutoff gesture, at which point the gasp abruptly stopped.

"Photon Guardians, you may not understand the significance of this. In addition to this planet, our ancestors at the same time inhabited M172. But uncontrolled strife on M172 led to a final battle to end all battles. It also ended all life."

"Bummer," mumbled Bhodi.

"Upon learning of the massive self-destruction of their sister planet, our ancestors immediately ceased all planetwide hostilities and labored to dispense with war and violence on our planet. Eventually they created the arena where disputes could be settled, sentient being to sentient being. And then, to guarantee that war would never again rear its ugly head, our scientists labored to create the great force field that protects us from all menaces."

Bhodi tapped Tivia on the arm and said in a low voice, "This guy doesn't strike me as an Emperor. He seems more like a game show host."

"What's a game show host?" asked Tivia.

"But enough of our history!" declared Emperor Flynn. "We have our seven lucky Photon Guardians to think about, and Catron, why don't you tell our guests what they've won!"

"Never mind," said Tivia. "I think I get the idea."

Catron rolled slightly forward, arms behind his back, as he thought cheerfully, "Well, Great One, the Photon Warriors, because of their unswerving dedication to the cause of the Light, have won an all-expense-paid vacation here to beautiful Dekka. They'll be guests at the luxurious Emperor's palace, be waited on hand and foot—or whatever," as he glanced at Pike's huge flipperlike extremities. "They will dine on the best food, have their choice of companionship from the most lovely or handsome of species we have on this planet, and . . ." He paused dramatically. "They'll also win this lovely set of Galactic Tourister luggage!"

A seven-piece set of luggage was rolled out on a cart by a lovely, red-skinned girl in a skimpy outfit. Bhodi's eyes widened when he saw her, but then he glanced at Tivia and decided to skip the wolf whistle he'd been about to give.

Leon stepped forward. "We very much appreciate your generosity, Emperor. I really don't know if it's proper for us to accept it . . ."

Now the Emperor's wide eyes narrowed, almost to slits, and his voice took on a silky, dangerous tone. "Of course it is. Are you implying that there's something wrong with my hospitality?"

"Not at all," said Leon. "But . . ."

"I must warn you"—now there was positive menace in the Emperor's voice—"that if you refuse my hospitality, you would insult me. Insulting the Emperor is against the laws of this planet, and matters could take a most . . . unfortunate turn."

There was dead silence throughout the court.

It was Tivia who stepped forward and bowed. "My dear Emperor, we are not diplomats. We are warriors. Please excuse any gaffes on our part as the actions of people much more accustomed to having their lives threatened rather than enriched."

The Emperor sat back and roared appreciatively. "Well spoken!" he exclaimed. "Well spoken indeed. Enough tension, my good friends. Now is a festive occasion. And because of that, let me bring out my second greatest treasures.'' He clapped his hands briskly, and a curtain at the far end of the throne room parted.

There was an expectant silence from the courtiers, for they knew exactly what was coming.

One at a time they came out, single file, looking neither left nor right. Large diaphanous robes swirled around them, giving tantalizing hints of their shapely figures. And, insanely, they all looked like the exact same girl, except in different stages of development. The girl in the lead was about seven years of age, and one by one as they passed through the curtain, the little girl seemed to grow up before their eyes. Eight, nine, ten, and as the years passed the same girl went from the clumsy awkwardness of adolescence to the smooth, confident walk of the teenager. The last girl in the line was about eighteen, and she was the only one who dared to look straight at the Photon Warriors.

Her skin was alabaster, her long hair red as autumn leaves. Her features were soft, no harsh angles or lines to any of them. She moved with an easy grace, and her eyes were large, like the Emperor's, and deepest blue.

She surveyed the Photon Guardians as she took her place at the end of the row of what was obviously her sisters. Bhodi felt his heart getting ready to rip free of his chest, scoot across the room and grovel in front of the eldest girl, begging, ''Use me as you will! Step on me, break me, I don't care! Just notice me!''

But even before such a disgusting organic event could occur, Bhodi immediately realized that he'd already been thrown out at first before he had even swung the bat. For when the girl made eye contact with Gambler, the electricity between the two of them was almost palpable. He looked at his friend and saw that Gambler's eyes had narrowed, his gaze consuming the young girl. And she was returning his attention with equally frank interest. Gambler's fist opened and clenched, the attraction between the two of them almost sending sparks leaping across the throne room.

Bhodi, in a low voice, said to his friend, "Will you turn it down? You're raising the temperature throughout the city."

Gambler, in an equally low voice, said, "Shhh. I'm working."

"Gentlemen and lady," thought out Catron the High Roller, "it is my honor to present the twelve daughters of the Emperor Flynn. Please meet," and he indicated from youngest to oldest, left to right, "Keaan, Kebben, Keccen, Kedden, Keeen, Keffen, Keggen, Kehhen, Keiin, Kejjen, Kekken and"—he paused before the eldest—"Kellen."

The Photon Guardians bowed slightly before them, but Gambler never removed his gaze from Kellen, nor she from him. He was jolted suddenly by Bhodi's elbow to the ribs.

"Will you get a grip on?" whispered Bhodi.

"I'm hoping to," shot back Gambler. Bhodi sighed in exasperation.

The Emperor stepped forward and walked down the line, touching each of his beloved daughters on the face with affection. "Are they not lovely?" he asked. "And each and every one a spitting image of her mother."

"May I ask, Emperor, where their mother is?" inquired Tivia.

"In retreat," he replied. "For some reason she hasn't let me near her in seven years. I have no idea why."

He put an arm around Kellen's shoulder. "Now I just want to warn you, should any of you get ideas . . ." And his smile lost all trace of humor. "Hands off my daughters. You may look to your heart's content, but you can't touch. They're mine."

Bhodi could feel Tivia next to him, bristling. He put a restraining hand on her forearm. "As you say, Emperor," agreed Bhodi evenly. And out of the side of his mouth he said to Tivia, "Later."

But on his other side Gambler was tugging at his sleeve. "Bhodi, she's got to be mine. Mine, we'll intertwine . . ."

"Later," hissed Bhodi.

A seething Tivia on the left, an eager Gambler on the right. Bhodi had one comforting thought. At least things couldn't get more complicated.

9
Things Get
More
Complicated

The Photon Guardians looked out the sides of the touring vehicle at the capital city of Dekka.

The buildings were opulent and splendid, everything from the domiciles and private homes to the office buildings and, naturally, the palace itself. The touring bus, which was long and shining and rode on a cushion of air, made a leisurely turn and headed in the direction of a tower that stood above the others. Bhodi had seen it earlier when they were outside of the city and voiced an interest in it now.

The tour guide was a short, shapeless creature that looked like nothing so much as a pile of Jell-O. Appendages grew out from it at will to faultlessly control the steering of the bus. A mouth appeared in the middle of its body as it said, "That is one of the force-field towers. There are twenty-five scattered throughout the planet, each projecting a shield over its own section of the planet. In the hundreds of years since we discovered the principle of the force field, nothing and no one has ever managed to break through. The actual mechanics of the force field is a closely guarded secret, for the concern is that if word got out as to how it was created, someone somewhere would figure out a way to break through it.''

Bhodi whistled, looking at the narrow tower. It stretched up and up, becoming narrower and narrower, and ended with a large projection disk on the top. It was so high that he had no clear idea just how large the projection disk was. "Boy," he said, "whoever runs those towers must have the cushiest job on Dekka."

"No one runs them," said the guide. "It's all fully automated. A limited number of people have access to the towers. It's all quite secure. No one even bothers to attack Dekka anymore. After all this time, sentients are starting to come to the realization that nothing can breach our defense."

Gambler spoke up. "So what you're saying is that, if you want a little privacy and can get in to one, you're not going to do better than a force-field tower."

"In essence, that is correct."

Gambler's innocent question went right past Bhodi and the rest of the Photon Warriors. Later they would be kicking themselves that they weren't listening more closely.

Along every block, Dekkans would stop and point and wave at the Photon Guardians. The Guardians, back in their normal garb once outside the palace, waved back. Bhodi said to Parcival, "Now I know how the President feels."

Parcival grinned widely. The young Photon Warrior was unused to this sort of attention, and was clearly enjoying it.

Pike, beneath half-lidded eyes, was watching the street carefully, keeping a look-out for any sign of Runya. He was upset that this relatively easy duty had been spoiled by the bad-tempered card-player. He was annoyed with himself as well, for he disliked the idea that anything from his personal life had spilled over into his duties as a Photon Warrior.

They rounded a corner and, as one, the Photon Guardians gasped.

The tour bus stopped and an arm oozed forth from their guide to wave proudly. "Our Emperor's prize possession," he said.

They stared at what was before them in rapt amazement. Tivia murmured, "I thought when he said his daughters were his second greatest treasure, he was just being arrogant. But . . ." and her voice trailed off.

Before them, a hundred feet tall, was one of the most magnificent sights they had ever seen.

"The Photon prism," announced the tour guide.

It stood there upright, towering over them with no visible means of support. It was a thousand times more beautiful than the most beautiful of Photon crystals. It was a perfectly cut, hundred-foot-high triangular prism, tall and glowing on its end. It caught the light from the sun and reflected it, breaking it into its component colors. The Photon Guardians were bathed in its light, their uniforms becoming patterns of gorgeous colors.

To their astonishment, it was Baethan who broke the silence. "It's magnificent."

It was an incredible pronouncement for the zealously unemotional cyborg to make, but there it was. And he spoke for them all. It was magnificent.

"Carved from pure Photonium before it fully crystallized," said the tour guide. "He had it created to celebrate the birth of his first daughter, Kellen. It has been the centerpiece of Dekka ever since."

"So I would imagine," said Pike.

It towered over them, radiating light and beauty, and they could think of nothing else to say, for truly there were no words to describe it.

The only one who was paying no attention was Gambler, who stared back at the force-field tower with a contemplative expression on his blue face.

Just before they angled back towards the palace, they passed an immense pit at least fifty yards wide. There were bleachers mounted all around. The floor of the pit was smooth and oddly decorated with red and green and yellow paint splotches, and a few other colors here and there. "What's that?" asked Tivia.

The guide looked across and said, "Sporting arena."

"Set in the ground?" asked Bhodi.

"How else?"

"Well, you could build a stadium. I mean, I don't see any doors down there. It must make it difficult for the teams to get in and out of the actual pit."

"Somewhat," agreed the guide, and then smoothly said, "There is the palace. The Emperor will be expecting you for dinner this evening."

"Wouldn't miss it," said Bhodi.

Bhodi had no idea what he ate that night. It all tasted good, but he had the distinct feeling that if he asked, he might not like the answers.

The others had been eagerly consuming the repast as well. Only Tivia and Baethan had been holding back, politely passing on any food that came their way. The Emperor, at the far end of the great table, called down, "I see that you are not eating, my friends. Is there any particular reason?"

Baethan, at his most dispassionate, said, "I am cyborg, Emperor. Consumption of food stuffs is foreign and meaningless to me. I would not deprive others by eating food that would only be wasted on me."

"Ah," said the Emperor, accepting the reason. He turned to Tivia. "And you, my dear?"

Tivia was silent for a moment and then gestured to her mask. "I would feel—self-conscious, Emperor."

"Nonsense!" said Flynn. "As you must be able to tell

from my city, my prism and my daughters, I have an appreciation for beauty. Remove the mask, Tivia. Share your beauty with us.''

Her eyes darted from one Guardian to another, searching for a graceful way out. Bhodi cleared his throat and said, ''Emperor, with all due respect, women of Tivia's planet customarily—''

''But she's not on her planet,'' said the Emperor, and now that dangerous tone was in his voice again. ''She's on mine, and while she's on mine, she'll play by my rules.''

And now Bhodi felt his temper starting to flare. Part of him warned that this was the most wrong thing he could do, but he ignored it. ''Now listen—''

And now it was Tivia who put a restraining hand on his arm. ''Bhodi, don't.''

''But—''

''It's all right. Really.'' She reached up and pulled her mask down.

Fascinated as he was by her rarely seen face, Bhodi couldn't help but stare at her in open admiration. The Emperor did as well. ''Now, why in the world,'' said Flynn, ''you would want to hide that lovely face from everyone is beyond me.'' He gestured to a steaming plate of food in front of her. ''Have you tried the cracked klava? It's truly excellent.''

Tivia picked up a thin prong and expertly speared a piece of the round, breaded klava, and popped it in her mouth. She chewed it for a moment and then smiled. Bhodi realized that he'd never seen her smile, and wished that he could see it more often.

''This is truly excellent,'' she said, and the Emperor laughed.

''Of course it is! Nothing but the best for my guests!''

Bhodi breathed a sigh of relief and caught Tivia's eye. She winked at him. He knew she regarded the removal of her mask as an invasion of her privacy, but all things considered she was taking it rather well.

He turned to his left to see how Gambler was doing and was stunned to see that his chair was empty.

He looked around and there, at the far end of the tables where the Emperor's daughters were seated, Gambler was directly behind Kellen and whispering in her ear. Merriment was etched on her face, and they both were casting sidelong glances at her father to make sure that he did not notice they were together.

On the other side of Gambler's seat was Leon. The lizoid warrior had noticed Gambler's whereabouts at about the same time that Bhodi had, and he started to rise from his place.

"No, Leon!" said Bhodi in a low, urgent whisper. "You've got the subtlety of a tank. The last thing we want to do is draw a lot of attention. Let me."

Bhodi waited until the right moment, when no one was paying attention to him, and then slowly eased away from his place. The Emperor was deeply engrossed in conversation with Tivia, and since he was Bhodi's main concern, Bhodi counted himself lucky.

Quietly he made his way across the room until he reached Gambler's side. Gambler didn't even notice him until Bhodi grabbed him firmly by the ear and hissed, "We're having words, Romeo."

"I'll be right back," said Gambler to the princess.

"No, he won't," said Bhodi, and pulled him quickly away.

They went into a narrow corridor and Bhodi tried not to explode. "Are you nuts? Are you stark-staring crazy? You heard Flynn. Hands off his daughters. This guy sounded flaky enough to have Tivia shot at sunrise if she didn't unmask. What do you think he's going to do to someone who's playing around with his daughters, specifically after he said not to."

"I'm not hitting on all the daughters," replied Gambler. "Just one, son."

"Just one. Look, Gambler, this guy is real important.

He exports all kinds of precious minerals and makes a fortune off it, but the thing that's most important to us is his supply of Photonium. Keep your hands to yourself, because you're holding the entire future of the Photon Alliance in them.''

Gambler put up his hands, palms out. "All right, all right! No need to get so intense. You say no touch, it's no touch. Okay? I mean, your friendship is important to me, Bhodi. More important than just one girl, no matter how gorgeous and well attached she is.''

Bhodi sighed with relief, glad that what he was saying appeared to be penetrating. "Okay. As long as we have that settled.''

"Besides, there's lots of action for a green-blooded young guy like me on this planet, right?'' He chuckled. "But don't worry. You've got Tivia all to yourself.''

"Thanks,'' said Bhodi.

They went back into the dining hall, and Bhodi gave Leon a quiet high-sign to indicate that everything was all right.

There were so many people as Flynn's guests that it was not until nearly the meal's end that Pike spotted Runya seated far away. He tapped Parcival on the shoulder and indicated the massive warrior, looking truly ludicrous in the ceremonial robes required at court. "Think I should say anything to him?'' asked Pike.

"Like what? 'Are you here for trouble?' ''

"Exactly, Parcival. Thank you, you always know just what to say.''

He was moving across the room before Parcival was able to make clear that he was only being sarcastic. He came out from behind the table and caught up to Pike just as, short arms on his hips, Pike demanded from Runya, "Are you here for trouble?''

Runya's twin heads looked up at Pike blandly. There was no menace in his eyes. "Why Pike—I don't know what you're talking about.''

Pike eyed him suspiciously. "What?"

"The Emperor has set the rules. No off-planet arguments to be brought onto Dekka. I shall live by that. I suggest you do the same."

"Well," said Pike uncertainly, "I'm glad that's settled."

"Yes." Runya smiled, but there was no warmth to the smile, and Pike slowly walked away. As he did so, Parcival made certain not to take his eyes off the towering Runya, as if concerned that he might launch some sort of attack. And indeed, he might have.

Night had fallen.

It had been the Photon Guardians' wish to leave that evening, but Flynn wouldn't hear of it. Besides the fact that he didn't wish the festivities to end, planetary tracking systems also indicated that three Arrian ships were now in orbit around Dekka. So leaving did not seem entirely possible anyway.

Each of the Photon Guardians had been given private quarters, and Bhodi lay back now, stretched out on the bed. It was bizarre for him to think that, as he lay here, back on Earth everyone was frozen into immobility. He wondered about the upward limit of MOM's abilities. After all, if she could freeze the Earth in this manner, was there any way she could cancel time around the Scarrcastle? The Warlord, frozen forever in time. Now there was a pleasant thought.

He rolled onto his stomach, his chin cupped between his hands. The more he thought about his life as a Photon Warrior, the more and more he started to realize that there were certain things that simply made no sense. Like that bad TV show he'd seen, there were fundamentals that just didn't hold up.

Why did the Warlord seem to have infinite capacity for Soldarrs and the like, and MOM's defense was entirely centered around the Photon Guardians? Why didn't the Warlord try to overwhelm Intellistar through sheer force of numbers and end the interference of the Photon Warriors once and for all? How did MOM always seem to know what the Warlord was planning and vice versa? They were always homing in on the same planet at the same time. It was as if . . .

. . . as if it were nothing more than a . . .

"Bhodi?"

He heard a soft voice behind him and almost didn't dare to turn around. When he did, he saw Tivia there. She still wore the long kaftan, and her mask was back in place. Her eyes glittered.

"I must be dreaming," he said.

She sighed in that impatient way of hers. "I was hoping to talk to you for a moment. But if you're going to be adolescent about it . . ."

"Me! Adolescent! No, nothing could be further from the truth. Come in, come in." He pulled a large pillow over for her to sit on and placed it next to him on the bed.

"No, thanks," she said warily and sat on the floor. She drew her knees up and laced her fingers around them. "Bhodi . . . how do you feel about me?"

He blinked. Gambler's words about "she's yours" came back to him. "Well, I . . . I think you're really great. That is, you're a great fighter and great ally, and I'm really glad that you're on our side. Because if you were one of the bad guys, I'd be very nervous about our chances of finally winning this war."

She blinked. "My mother has been uneasy about my joining the Photon Guardians."

"Really?" He leaned on one elbow. "I guess I can understand that. If I had even told my mother, she would have freaked."

"But only because she would be concerned for your safety. My mother is quite certain that I can take care of myself. Her concern was that constant exposure to males would possibly dilute my sense of purpose."

"Which, translated, means that she's afraid you're going

to break your planet's cardinal rule and actually like guys.
Is that it?''

She nodded. ''That's it.''

There was a pause, and he asked in a low voice, ''Has
it?''

She didn't make an immediate reply. Then she said, her
normally strong voice barely above a whisper, ''Remember you said, about the war being over? About if we ever
won, completely and decisively?''

''Yeah?''

''Well . . .'' she cleared her throat, ''I don't know if I'd
ever want that to happen.''

He laughed incredulously. ''Why not?''

''Because if it did, there would be no real reason to
keep the Photon Guardians together. So if we disbanded
. . . I'd probably never see you again.''

His breath caught as he leaned forward. ''Well, don't
I irritate you? Wouldn't it be nice never to have to put up
with me again?''

She huffed. ''Yes, of course you irritate me. And
I'd . . .''

''You'd what?''

''I'd . . . miss it.''

He reached towards her then, and he didn't think she
was going to pull away . . .

And at that moment a shout sounded throughout the
palace.

''We're under attack!'' snapped Bhodi, and he automatically grabbed for his phaser. It wasn't there. All their
weapons were in safekeeping.

Tivia leaped to her feet as did Bhodi. Tivia looked at
him and her eyes widened. ''Bhodi . . .''

He looked down. ''Whoops.'' He grabbed the blanket
up around himself. ''Meet you out there.''

''Right.''

Seconds later Bhodi was running down the hallway after
Tivia, tying the kaftan around himself as he went. Guests

were pouring out and into the main throne room, which was where the shouts were originating from.

One of the house servants was there, a thin, gangly creature with a huge nose. It was lying under a table yelling the same thing over and over, and when Bhodi got close enough he heard the word, "Trespass!"

The Emperor lumbered forth, rubbing the sleep from his eyes. He hauled the houseman to his feet and shook him briskly. "What's going on? What are you shouting about? You've awakened all the guests."

"Trespass, your majesty," stammered the houseman. "I was walking through the throne room on my rounds when I saw a quick motion of someone coming out of there."

He pointed to a curtained-off doorway and the Emperor blanched. "The entrance to my daughters' rooms," he thundered. "Who was it?"

"I don't know, your majesty. It was so dark, what with the lights off, I couldn't quite see. He was about as tall as I, I think, although he might have been hunched over as he ran. He darted behind the throne and, as I moved to turn on the lights, he came up behind me and knocked me out. When I woke up, I was under this table, and that's when I sounded an alarm."

The Emperor turned on his guests. "All right," he said, a murderous tone in his voice. "Who was it? I assure you, the longer you endeavor to hide, the greater will be my anger, and the more fearful the punishment. Which one of you was dallying with my daughter against my strict instructions?"

Bhodi surveyed the room, and several yards away he caught sight of Gambler. Gambler put a finger to his lips to indicate that Bhodi should keep silent, and Bhodi felt all the blood drain from his face. That idiot! How could he have . . .

Catron rolled towards the Emperor and thought, "Do you wish me to scan for the guilty party, Lord Emperor?"

"No," said the Emperor firmly. "There are ways to

deceive telepaths, Catron. Ways for those guilty to block their thoughts, or for those who are innocent to be nervous about some other affront and thus bear false witness against themselves. Besides—we have laws to cover this.'' His face crinkled in expectation. ''Oh, yes. Laws.''

At that moment a voice boomed forth. ''I cannot keep silent on this any longer.''

Everyone turned as Runya strode forth, towering a head higher (and wider) than anybody else in the place. In slow, measured tones, he rumbled, ''I saw the entire thing. I was restless, walking around the palace, and came upon the throne room just as the perpetrator was throwing his victim under the table.''

''He was as I described him?'' said the houseman.

''Yes and no.''

The Emperor looked fit to be tied. ''What do you mean, yes and no? Speak plainly. Did you see who it was?''

''Certainly. You see, when the houseman saw him, he was slim and agile. But that was merely a disguise.''

''Disguise?'' asked the Emperor.

''Yes. He thought he was unobserved, so after he knocked out the houseman, he resumed his normal shape.''

He pointed straight across the room. ''It was Pike.''

Pike stifled a laugh. ''Don't be absurd. With all due respect, your Emperorness, your daughters wouldn't hold any interest for me. We're not even the same species. I would be as attracted to them as you would be to a fish.''

It was precisely the wrong thing to say. Slowly the Emperor approached him until he was eye to eye with Pike. ''Are you implying,'' he said in a low, angry tone, ''that my daughters are as attractive as fishes?''

''No. Not at all. It's just that . . .''

''*Be silent!*'' his infuriated command echoed throughout the throne room. ''You have been accused, Photon Guardian. Accused of breaking the law. And you must answer your accuser in the manner of our planet. Trial by combat!''

The crowd took up the shout. "Trial by combat! Trial by combat!"

Bhodi moaned softly to himself. Things had indeed gotten more complicated.

10

Death Before Dishonor

A huge procession, with Pike and Runya at the head, moved outdoors heading for the arena that the Warriors had seen earlier that day. The temperature had dropped substantially at night, and the billowing kaftans everyone was wearing certainly didn't help matters.

Parcival and Leon were desperately trying to talk sense into the Emperor, but he wasn't remotely interested in listening. He was far too caught up in the excitement of the moment. Even the slight to his daughters had taken a back seat in his mind to the pageantry of the trial.

At the head of the crowd, prodded by heavily armed guards, Runya and Pike were pushed along. Pike was trying to convince the guards that this was all complete nonsense, that Runya had merely taken advantage of a situation to try and settle his own grudge.

Bhodi cut as fast as he could through the crowd, shoving beings aside and being roundly cursed out, until he finally found who he was looking for. He grabbed Gambler from behind and spun him around. "Look, this has gone too far!" he snapped. "Pike's in real trouble."

Gambler kept walking. "I'll say he is. Sneaking in on the Emperor's daughters. That's pretty incredible."

For a moment Bhodi just stammered, unable to get the words out. "Of course it's incredible! He didn't do it. You did!"

"Shush!" He turned and faced Bhodi. The crowd continued marching around them. "You'd better watch what you say. You could get me in serious trouble with accusations like that."

"Serious trouble?!" screeched Bhodi. "Pike's about to go one-on-one with someone who could drop-kick a battle cruiser, and you're concerned about serious trouble?" He grabbed Gambler by the front of his gown. "*This* is serious! If it gets any *more* serious, it's going to be a funeral."

In low, intense tones Gambler said, "Look, Bhodi. You told me to keep hands off the girl. I kept hands off the girl. Now someone else goes playing fast and loose, and you're all over me. Well, look elsewhere for your man, Stan. It's not me." He pulled away from the astonished Bhodi Li.

Bhodi stood there. "You're really not going to say anything, are you?"

"There's nothing to say, except let's go and root for Pike." And then he had rejoined the crowd and marched away from Bhodi.

By the time Bhodi got to the front of the crowd, they had already reached the arena. He got there just in time to see Pike and Runya being lowered via huge slings into the bottom of the pit. Once they got there, the slings were withdrawn, and Bhodi realized with a jolt why it was preferable that people within the arena found it difficult to leave.

"Sporting arena, my eye," he said to Baethan. "We have to do something."

"There is nothing we can do," said Baethan. "To

handle a crowd of this size we would most definitely need our weapons, and they are simply not here. Remember, though, that Pike is a Photon Warrior. All things being equal, he should be able to triumph.''

''All things being equal?'' He pointed at Runya who stood waiting at one side of the arena. ''That guy is built like the Intellistar. He could eat a dozen Pikes for breakfast.''

''Putting aside the questionable nutritional aspects of your statement, I consider size to be an irrelevant factor. Patience, Bhodi Li. Patience.''

Bhodi leaned over the edge of the arena, which was surrounded by a wall about four feet high. The bleachers were already starting to fill up, and there were angry shouts to Bhodi of ''Down in front!'' and ''Out of the way.'' Bhodi shook his head. Hero one day, obstruction the next. He stayed where he was.

The other Photon Guardians lined up next to him. It was clear that although they had confidence in Pike as a war-rior, they were still nervous about the seemingly unbeat-able foe he was about to face. Bhodi looked at Parcival—he knew Pike the best and Bhodi looked to him for guidance to Pike's real chances. But Parcival's face was unreadable. Whatever anxiety he was feeling, he had deliberately closed it out. Likewise with the others. Finally he looked at Gambler, but Gambler refused to return his gaze.

Then Bhodi took another look at the paint stains on the base of the arena, and with a sick realization he knew that they were not paint at all. They were stains from blood of various creatures.

Emperor Flynn stood high on a podium nearby, and when he spoke, his voice reverberated, seemingly from one end of the city to the other.

''My people!'' he called. ''As we have had so many times before, there is before you an accused. And an accuser. I'd like to introduce them to you now. On the left, he's a Photon Guardian. He's a warrior. He fights for the Light. And, unless he was fooling around with my daughters, he's a heck of a nice sentient being. Let's have a big Dekkan welcome for Pike the Foppo!''

There was wild applause from all around. Someone abruptly came up behind Bhodi, a surly individual who said, ''Move it or lose it.''

Bhodi swung smoothly, a hard right to the jaw, and the surly individual dropped like a stone. ''No,'' said Bhodi to the unconscious form.

''And on the other side of the arena,'' the Emperor was continuing, ''you know him. You've gambled with him. You've probably lost to him. And now he's in for the big game as he stands as Pike's accuser. Let's have a big round of applause for Runya the Genevan!''

There was applause again but this time mixed with catcalls and hisses. For some reason Bhodi took comfort in that.

''Rule one—no weapons,'' intoned the Emperor. ''Rule two—no pooftas.''

''What's a poofta?'' asked Bhodi.

''Pooftas. It's a Dekkan word,'' said Baethan. ''It means betting.''

''Rule three—no rule three,'' said the Emperor. ''In fact, no more rules. The one who's left standing, wins.''

''Left standing,'' said Parcival. ''That's encouraging. So Pike may not have to kill him. Just incapacitate him.''

Tivia nodded. ''Of course, we have no assurance that Runya is going to use any such restraint.''

Slowly Pike and Runya approached each other, circling warily. Pike was no longer trying to talk Runya out of this course of action. He knew it had gone much too far for that. His arms outstretched, his feet braced, he waited for Runya's move while running through his mind everything that Runya was likely to do.

With a roar, Runya charged. He took three steps, four and then left his feet. Incredibly agile for one so huge, he aimed a vicious sidekick straight at Pike's huge head.

Pike leaped to one side and rolled across the smooth

ground. Runya landed, stomping down on nothing, but he turned lightning fast and was upon Pike before the Photon Warrior could stand. Wrapping three arms around the front of Pike's head, he put his fourth hand behind Pike's head and started to push forward. Pike groaned from the strain.

Parcival screamed, "He's trying to break his neck! Somebody, do something!"

Unarmed as they were, nevertheless the Photon Warriors started to clamber over the guard rail, prepared to jump down into the pit fifty feet below. Suddenly the Emperor's guards appeared all around them, armed to the teeth. They froze, knowing that if they moved even an inch farther they'd be paralyzed or worse.

At that moment there was a scream from down in the pit. But it wasn't Pike who was doing the screaming. Runya was howling, gasping at a dozen holes in his tough skin. And Pike was standing there, grinning, foot-long spikes protruding from his clothes.

"He changed into one of those creatures from the Maniller galaxy," shouted Leon. "What're those called . . . Quillers!"

"Of course!" said Parcival. "It's a Quiller from Maniller. Good going, Pike!"

Pike waved, and then he started to run towards the staggering Runya. Even as he moved, his body started to ripple and change. His mass reshaped itself once again, his body becoming rock hard, his upper torso shifting into an inverted triangle. His head flattened down and became almost nonexistent. His legs became longer, picking up speed with every step.

Runya turned and saw him coming but was too slow to get out of the way. Having metamorphosed into a full-blown Charger, Pike rammed into him with all his strength. The momentum of the charge lifted Runya completely off his feet, and they kept on going until Pike smashed him against the wall with a bone-jarring crunch.

He backed away, shapeshifting again as Runya staggered forward. Runya drove a heavy fist into Pike's chest and, to his astonishment, he penetrated easily and kept on going. Pike had become little more than a walking blob, and the moment Runya let up the pressure, his fist snapped back out and hit him in the left face.

The Photon Guardians howled and cheered. "I wasn't worried," said Parcival. "Not for a minute."

Runya staggered to his feet, trying desperately to clear his heads. Pike hung back, having assumed his normal shape. "Give up, Runya," he said, "before you wind up really getting hurt."

At that moment a small, fast-moving alien leaped to the top of the guard rail and hurled down a small sack into the pit. It landed on the ground with a thud.

Pike had not been expecting it, but Runya clearly had. Before Pike could make a move, Runya had covered the distance and grabbed up the bag. He ripped it open and pulled out a pair of disintegrator guns.

"Uh oh," muttered Pike, and he backed up quickly.

Runya advanced on him. "You'll die for what you did to me, Pike!"

"Now now," said Pike, backing up and aware the entire time that he was coming up to the wall. "Let's not be hasty about this. After all, you're breaking the rules."

"Of course I'm breaking the rules!" said Runya. "I do it all the time. All I wanted was you, Pike! I wasn't going to miss my opportunity."

Pike halted, back against the wall. "That's why you lied about seeing me coming out of the—"

"Of course I lied! I'll take any opportunity to kill you, Pike. You disgraced me."

"You disgrace yourself," said Pike.

"And you're dead." He raised one of the disintegrators. "Die, Pike!"

"No!" shouted Parcival, and this time Bhodi, Baethan, Leon and Tivia were leaping over the barrier, sliding and tumbling down the sheer walls into the pit. Guards took aim at them, but Gambler lit into them, knocking their weapons from their hands and moving like a blur.

But it was all too slow. Runya fired. There was a dazzling flash of light from his disintegrator . . .

And where Pike had been standing a moment ago, now there was nothing but a huge pile of ash.

11

Phoenix

"*Pike!*" screamed Parcival, and he too leaped down into the arena, tumbling down the sloping, smooth walls.

Gambler halted, about to throw a punch, and looked down in dismay. His eyes were wide with shock, and then he didn't see anything as one of the guards took the opportunity and knocked him out from behind. Gambler went down, slumping unconscious to the floor.

Below, in the pit, the Photon Guardians slowly approached Runya. He waved his disintegrators at them, and they halted, but there was murder in their eyes.

"You won't escape, Runya," grated Leon. "Not them," pointing to the guards, "and not us. Maybe they're under instructions not to interfere with what goes on in this pit, but we're not under any such instructions."

"You set him up!" wailed Parcival. "How could you do it?"

"All right, all of you get back," snarled Runya, waving his disintegrator at Parcival, "or otherwise the squirt gets it first."

At that moment, the ashes behind Runya made a noise.
He glanced back with one head, and the one head couldn't believe what its one eye was seeing.

The bird's head emerged first. The golden plumed head, the razor-sharp beak poked from the ashes and let out a spine-chilling cry. Then the long, beautiful neck, and added into the golden plumage were feathers of scarlet.

It came faster then, this magnificent bird. From the ashes it grew, wings spanning ten feet across, talons to rip and shred, feathers glistening off the lights that surrounded the arena. It stood before Runya in all its glory and shrieked, a high, ululating scream.

Runya's hands, all four of them, shook uncontrollably. He tried to stammer out something, anything.

The great bird drew back its right wing and swung it around. It smashed into Runya with the impact of a pile driver, knocking his heads together and stunning him momentarily.

The bird shifted again, and now it was no longer a bird. Its legs became short and stubby, and all of its bodily mass went into the creation of two massive arms, made of solid muscle, with fists the size of boulders. The rest of its body was thick, heavy, cylindrical and brown. Its legs were little more than nubs and two beady eyes peered out from the top of its tubelike body.

It stepped close and delivered a massive wallop to Runya's heads. Its arms swung back and forth, delivering one haymaker after another onto the hapless Runya. Runya staggered back, tried to mount a defense, failed miserably.

Leon recognized the creature first. "It's a Punching Bogg!" he chortled.

The Punching Bogg kept slamming away. One of Runya's heads was now totally unconscious. His movements were stiff and sluggish, he couldn't focus or bring his strength to bear.

There was a long moment when the Punching Bogg

hesitated, and at that moment, Runya, through swollen lips and broken teeth, said, "Please . . . don't . . ."

"Should have thought of that earlier," said the Punching Bogg. It drew back its huge right arm and, putting every ounce of strength in its body behind it, smashed a roundhouse blow to Runya's head. Runya pivoted in place like a broken top, and then slowly began to topple over.

"Tiiiiimber!" shouted Bhodi, and stepped back to give Runya space.

The four-limbed alien fell flat on his faces with a huge "whumpf," and lay still.

A deafening roar went up from the spectators. The Punching Bogg stepped back and slowly began to shift again. Although it was obvious who it was, nevertheless the Photon Warriors held their breath until the being in front of them had completely shifted into its more customary form.

"Pike!" shouted Parcival joyously. He ran to the round Photon Guardian and embraced him. His arms didn't come close to reaching completely around, but that didn't matter. None of it mattered. "You're alive," he choked. "You're alive!"

Pike patted him on the back. "Well, of course I am. You didn't think a blundering oaf like him could finish me off, did you?"

"But how?" said Bhodi. "We saw him disintegrate you, reduce you to ashes."

Pike shook his head. "A moment before he fired, I changed myself into a Phoenix at the start of its life cycle."

"A Phoenix," said Bhodi.

Trying to compose himself, Parcival took refuge in reciting facts that he had at his fingertips. "The Phoenix is a birdlike creature native to Antos 3," he said. "It's believed to be the basis for the legends of the Phoenix throughout the galaxy. It lives for a hundred years, then reduces itself to ashes, only to rise from those same ashes moments later."

"Exactly," said Pike.

"A logical maneuver," Baethan said crisply. "A wonder that it did not occur to me."

"Maybe you were worried," Leon suggested, pounding Pike on the back. "You gave us a scare there, Pike. Next time find some way to let us know you're okay."

"Maybe I'll let the ashes fall into the word 'Hi' next time," suggested Pike.

It was some time later when everyone was assembled in the main throne room again. Runya, all his arms in energized manacles, was just starting to come around. The Photon Warriors had assembled there, and that was when Bhodi realized that Gambler was nowhere to be seen.

On his throne, Emperor Flynn was at the height of his imperiousness. "Runya," he intoned, "you have borne false witness against Pike. This was against the laws of this planet. Further, you had an accomplice give you weapons during a trial by combat. This alone would have been enough to exonerate Pike had he not actually managed to beat you. However the case may be, Pike, through trial of combat, is hereby declared innocent of all charges. Runya, you shall be placed in protective custody until such time as it is convenient to have you transported off-planet. Since you are not a native Dekkan, you will merely be banished. You are never to set foot on our planet again, or you will suffer dearly for it."

Runya moaned in reply and was pulled unresisting out of the throne room.

The Emperor turned to Pike. "You have been fully cleared and exonerated of any charges against you, Pike—although I still can't say I'm wild about the fish crack."

"Sorry, your highness," said Pike gravely.

"Hm. Yes. Still, we are left wondering who my houseman saw coming out of my daughters' wing. But, no matter, I suppose. Certainly all of this will have shown him that he's playing a dangerous game, and that there would be serious consequences should he continue." He nodded to all assembled. "Believe it or not, my good friends, it's still the middle of the night. I suggest we all get back to sleep and start afresh in the morning. That's all."

The Photon Warriors went their separate ways, several clapping Pike on the back purely in their pleasure at seeing him still alive. Just before he retired, the Emperor said to Pike. "You know, when all is said and done—that was a marvelously good show you gave us."

Pike inclined his large head, "Anytime, your highness. But hopefully not anytime soon."

The Emperor laughed loudly at that and went off to bed.

Bhodi stood there for a long moment and watched Tivia go off to her own quarters. He knew she would not be coming back that night, and possibly not any night in the future. There had been a moment there, but the moment was gone and Bhodi sighed for the lost possibilities.

Just outside his quarters, he heard sobbing.

He paused, listening, trying to figure out who it might be, and then he realized and entered.

There was Gambler, his chest heaving, glistening tears streaming down his cheeks. He looked up, saw Bhodi and immediately went to him, grabbing him by the front of his kaftan and soaking it with his tears.

"I'm so suh-sorry," he wailed. His whole body shook with racking sobs. "I thought Pike was dead and it was all because of muh-me."

Sternly Bhodi said, "I think that Pike is the one you should be apologizing to, don't you?"

"I can't . . ."

"You have to." He paused. "You were the one coming out of the princesses' rooms, weren't you?" It was not a question.

"Yes," said Gambler between sniffles. "Aw, Bhodi, she's gorgeous, man. Kellen is just incredible. She—"

"I don't want to hear it, Gambler."

"Look," said Gambler desperately. "I didn't mean any harm by it. Really. Haven't you ever had a girl whose father disapproved of you? And you found yourself sneaking around just so you could see her?"

Bhodi thought about Cheryl Ann Chapel's father, who had called him a bum and threatened to sic the dogs on him. He had loved sneaking off with Cheryl Ann to the woods and making out like a bandit. When Cheryl Ann had wound up ditching him for Pete Wanamaker, it had annoyed him not only because he liked her, but also because he couldn't do something that annoyed her officious father anymore.

"Okay, yeah," said Bhodi. "But that was different. There's a lot riding on this. And you kept your mouth shut and let Pike take the rap for it."

"I was scared, man!" wailed Gambler. "Scared for myself, scared for Kellen. It all seemed so harmless. I never thought it would snowball the way that it did. It was a mistake, Jake. A big, stupid mistake."

"I can't just let it slide, Gambler," said Bhodi. "I have to at least tell Leon—"

Gambler grabbed desperately at his arm. "No. Oh, please don't. They'll throw me out for sure."

"Maybe not."

"You're my friend, man. You said so. Friends stick up for each other. Just cut me some slack, Jack. I swear, I'll fly straight and narrow from now on. Swear to Kolker, man, I will. Just please, not a word. Please. Please."

Bhodi felt a choking in his throat. "You've really learned your lesson?"

"Oh, absolutely. I'm not getting within a hundred kilometers of Kellen. She does something to me, turns me inside out. You know, like how you must feel with Tivia."

"Oh, don't talk to me about Tivia, Gambler. The perfect moment, ruined because of your rotten timing."

Gambler's scarlet eyes gleamed. "Tell me."

"No." Bhodi pulled away from him and plunked down on the bed. "It's private."

"Give, give," said Gambler, grinning. "You gotta tell me everything."

So Bhodi did, and when he got to how he started to reach for Tivia when the shouting abruptly started, Gambler moaned as if shot through with an arrow. "Oh, I am sorrier now than I was before. So near and yet so far."

"Well, look, if it's going to happen, it'll happen," said Bhodi philosophically. "Get to bed, Gambler. We'll be shoving off tomorrow afternoon, and no one's gotten much rest so far tonight."

"You bet." He stood, headed towards the door, then stopped and turned. "Promise you won't tell," he said, genuinely concerned. "It would kill me to get tossed out."

"Scout's honor," said Bhodi Li, and he made the Boy Scout gesture. Gambler returned the salute and left.

Bhodi lay back on his bed. All right. Gambler had made a stupid mistake, and it almost cost all of them. Then again, Bhodi had made his share of stupid mistakes and had frequently had to be pulled out of bad situations. Gambler had gotten himself in deep and had had no idea how to get out from under. So he had been lucky. Pike had settled Runya's hash, and everything had sorted itself out. Gambler had learned a valuable lesson, and ultimately, no one had been hurt. Just this one time, Bhodi could keep his secret. After all, he was supposed to be Gambler's friend.

Gambler walked out into the hallway, then turned and sagged against the wall. He let out a long breath. Then he ran the conversation back in his mind and marveled at it.

"What a sucker," he said with a soft laugh. "Oh, Gambler, you got him eating out of the palm of your hand."

12
Breach of Faith

"How much longer do we wait here?" demanded Mandarr.

Warriarr studied the shining orb of Dekka beneath them. "As long as it takes," he said. "How many Soldarrs do we have on all three ships combined?"

"One hundred and fifty three, plus the six of us," said Mandarr. He leaned forward over the viewscreen and snarled at the planet. "All we need is one break and we can tear the planet apart," he said.

Bugarr, who had come up behind them, said, "Quite right. Since war is obsolete on their planet, they have virtually no weaponry to speak of. Crack their defensive shield and they are ours."

Warriarr considered the situation and then flipped a toggle switch on the communications board. "Full power to weapons. I want to take another shot at that shield. Concentrate fire at"— he consulted an array of figures— "zero-zero-nine-mark-twelve."

There was a brief flickering of lights as all but emergency power was rerouted. A Soldarr's voice sounded over the intercom. "We await your command."

"Fire," said Warriarr.

Power surged forth from the phaser cannons under the Dark Destroyer. It created a dazzling and sustained display as it hit the barrier and went no further.

Warriarr maintained fire for half a minute before he ordered a cessation. "Mandarr, any sign of buckling by the shield?"

Mandarr leaned over his sensor equipment. "Not the slightest," he said. There did not seem to be any trace of sorrow in his voice.

"You like to see me fail, don't you?" said Warriarr.

Mandarr smiled unabashedly. "Yes."

Before Warriarr could reply, a Soldarr spoke again on the intercom. "Warriarr, engineers on all three ships inform us that maintaining full battle readiness for such a lengthy period of time is causing a drain on our power and resources. No ship is prepared to be ready for battle for days at a time."

Warriarr considered this. "All right. Bring down the shields. They don't have any planet-to-space defense system anyway. Cut life support to minimum. Power down weapons until they're needed."

"Yes, sir."

Almost immediately lights went to half strength inside the ship. The instrument board lights started to go off, one by one. Mandarr surveyed the development with distaste. "And what does all of this mean?" he demanded.

"It means," Warriarr said reasonably, "we sit around and wait some more."

"This is ridiculous," snarled Mandarr. "I know. Why don't we jump into hyperspace? The shield won't exist in hyperspace. And we'll come out of it inside of the shield. Then we can lay waste to the planet and those cursed Photon Guardians."

"Impossible," Bugarr spoke up. "We'd never be able

to stop in time once we got out of hyperspace. By the time we corrected our course and speed we will have hit the planet and gone halfway to the core.''

"But there must be a way!" cried Mandarr. "There has to be."

"There is," said Warriarr. "There is. It's called patience. The only virtue that I possess. I'd suggest you practice it as well."

He studied the planet surface again. "Sun's coming up. Bugarr, maintain sensor scan. We have to be ready on a moment's notice." He was silent for a time and then, in his low menacing voice, he said, "It's morning down there. I wonder what our Photon Guardians are up to."

"Keeps you fit, Bhodi. You should do it every morning."

Leon lumbered ahead of him, breathing in the fresh morning air. He was in his full Photon armor, as was Bhodi. Far in the distance the capital of Dekka gleamed in the morning sun.

"You know," Bhodi huffed behind him, "jogging is real big on Earth."

"Jogging?" said Leon. "It just never hurts to brush up on your basic retreating. Putting distance between yourself and your opponent is always a handy knack to have."

Bhodi drew next to him and they trotted next to each other for a time. Then, in a carefully neutral voice, Leon said, "Bhodi Li, if Gambler told you that he was the one who was sneaking around with the Emperor's daughters, you would tell me, wouldn't you?"

"Of course," said Bhodi quickly. Maybe a little too quickly, he thought to himself.

If Leon thought so as well, he didn't say. "Gambler's a good warrior. A good friend, to you in particular. But sometimes his judgment's cloudy. I can tell these things, and no matter how good he is, if he can't act in the best interests of all concerned, he'll have to go. You understand that, don't you, Bhodi?"

"Sure, sure," said Bhodi easily. "Although you've got to admit that I've done some less than brilliant things in my career as well."

"Sure you have." Ground crunched under his massive feet. "But whenever you did, it was with the intention of benefiting everyone on the team. You thought you were doing it in our best interests, even if you did pick a reckless way to go about it. That's okay. It's simply the mark of an inexperienced but talented soldier. Now, Gambler, on the other hand . . ."

Bhodi drew up short, snapping up the visor on his helmet. "What about Gambler?" he said angrily. "If you've got something to say about him, then spit it out."

Unperturbed, Leon said, "My only concern is that Gambler might be out mostly for himself. That he'll put his personal wants and needs above the greater good. That's dangerous, and it can get us all killed."

His breath misted in front of him, and Bhodi said, "You're wrong. That's all, Leon. You're just plain wrong, okay? Maybe you don't trust Gambler, but I do." He snapped the visor back down and started running. "I'd trust him with my life."

The young couple made their way through the streets of Dekka. They glanced neither right nor left and kept their faces huddled together so no one could see them clearly. Their long capes obscured their bodies, and since they did nothing overt, there were none to pay them any particular heed.

Their destination loomed in front of them—the great tower that projected part of the planetwide shield. There was a large service entrance but the door was seamlessly locked. There was, however, a small slit in the door itself.

"Now, are you sure your father will never miss it?" asked Gambler in a low tone.

Kellen giggled, that musical laughter that made Gambler's blood boil. From inside her large hood she said,

"Don't worry. He comes out here once in a blue moon. There's no need for concern." She kissed him on the cheek. "Trust me."

He grinned widely. "I do. Believe me, I do."

As she pulled a small, flat card out from the folds of her cloak, she said, "You know, I've never done this before. I've never done anything that my father wouldn't want me to do."

"Oh, I don't believe that," Gambler chided her.

"Weeeelll." She waved her head from side to side as she slid the card in. "Okay. Little stuff. Teeny tiny stuff he'd never find out about or even care about, really. But this, this is big time."

"Welcome to living dangerously, Kellen," he said. "That's where I like it. Life on the edge, life in the fast lane."

She giggled again, not understanding everything that Gambler was talking about and not caring all that much. All she knew was that Gambler was easily the most exciting boy she had ever met, and the disapproval that her father would feel for what she was doing only added spice to her adventure.

After all, she reasoned, the worst that would happen to Gambler was that her father would have him executed. The worst that would happen to her was that she would be sent to her room. So Gambler was taking all the risk as far as she was concerned, which was how he seemed to like it.

She wondered distantly, if Gambler were executed, would it bother her? She decided it probably wouldn't. He was nice, exciting, but sometimes a little too uppity for his station in life.

The door computer analyzed the encoded message on the card and slid the door open obediently. Kellen pulled out the card, and she and Gambler walked into the tower. The door hissed shut behind them.

Once the door closed they were assaulted by the noise of the machinery. Gambler looked around him—the wall was

covered with cabinets that hummed with the power necessary
to maintain the shielding, and all the instruments required to
monitor and maintain it. Covering his sensitive ears, Gambler shouted, "Is there any place quieter than this?"

She gestured downward, towards a set of spiral stairs.
They went down them, and pounding and humming sounds
receded ever so slightly as they entered the bowels of the
tower.

When they had gone as far down as they could go,
Gambler gallantly removed his cloak and laid it on the
ground. She did as well and they looked at each other for
a long moment, gazes locked. She smiled enticingly,
and then he grabbed her with clumsy eagerness and pulled
her down to the ground.

All around them the machinery came to life.

Gambler, with his extra-sensitive hearing, screamed as
he was assaulted by the cacophony around him. He hunched
over, his brain screaming for release. It was like being
caught in a bell tower with a ceaseless, unrelenting pounding of sound.

Kellen was not in quite as bad shape, but she was
uncomfortable nevertheless. "Gambler, let's find somewhere else!" she called as loudly as she could. But Gambler couldn't hear her, the sounds of the heavy machinery
around him eating away at his brain.

Everything had been ruined. He had been looking forward to this assignation all night and now it was falling
apart. What incredibly rotten luck.

"No!" he shouted. "Gamblers make their own luck!"

He lurched towards the vast array of wall machinery, all
incomprehensible to him. All he knew was that if he shut
down some of these incredibly noisy contraptions, he
might actually have some time to turn his attention to
Kellen.

He started pulling down on all the switches and pushing
all the buttons that he could find. He pulled dozens of
levers, looking for some way of removing the oppressive

noise from his head. Kellen was shouting something at him, but he paid no attention, his single-minded purpose overwhelming everything.

He found one last, huge red lever and pulled on it. At first it refused to budge, but then it snapped downward with a huge "k-chunk." The noise reverberated through the room like the final thud of a guillotine blade.

The noise stopped.

And into the void came Kellen's voice in midsentence, "—op it! Don't touch those—"

All at once a warning Klaxon began to sound. Gambler looked around, wild-eyed. "What's that?"

"The alarm!" shrieked Kellen, wringing her hands. "You dropped the force field. We're unprotected for the first time in centuries. Bring it up or my dad's going to kill us!"

Bugarr sprang to his feet. "Warriarr!" he shouted. "There's a hole in the force field!"

"It's a trick!" snarled Mandarr.

"Or an opportunity," shot back Warriarr. "We can't afford to let it pass." He hit the ship-to-ship intercom. "All power to engines! We're going in."

Pirarr's voice crackled over the intercom. "Are ye sure about all power to—"

"Now!" shouted Warriarr.

Single file, the three Dark Destroyers plunged downward towards the hole. The gap was there, highlighted in glowing green on the computer screen, and there were three blips representing the ships. Mandarr watched them through narrow eyes. "We won't make it," he said with utter certainty, then closed his eyes against the impact.

"Approaching," said Warriarr relentlessly. "Five . . . four . . . three . . . two . . . one . . ."

The ships leaped into the atmosphere of Dekka.

"We're through!" howled Warriarr. "The Darkness grows! Ahhhh-ha-aha-ha-ha-ha!"

Like a swarm of locusts, the three ships plummeted towards the surface of Dekka.

The Klaxon had spread throughout the city, warnings screaming throughout to all the citizenry. It had been so long since there had been any sort of alarm through the city of Dekka that many people didn't know what was going on.

The Emperor, who was sharing a leisurely breakfast with Tivia and Pike, leaped to his feet, his face a study of twisted rage. "We've been breached! The force field has failed." He slid down his sleeve to reveal a wrist communication device. He punched in a code number and shouted into it, "Central Control! What in the name of Kolker is going on?"

Central Control, who oversaw all the comings and goings of everything throughout the city of Dekka, responded frantically, "Readings indicate a mechanical failure in Force-field Generator A."

"That's our generator!" snapped the Emperor. "Do something."

"We're sending men over t—hold it! It's been brought back up! It's repaired itself," he said in absolute bafflement, and then his bafflement turned to near panic. "Emperor! Planetary sensors indicate that the three Arrian ships previously orbiting have come through the temporary hole." His voice choked. "We're under attack. Computers indicate that they will reach planet surface in under two minutes."

Forcing himself to remain calm, the Emperor said, "Projected landing point?"

There was a brief pause as whoever was answering on the other end did quick calibrations. "The capital city, sir. Us."

"There!" Gambler shoved the last of the switches back into their previous positions. The machinery was going at

full roar, but the Klaxon had not ceased sounding.
Gambler looked around frantically and slammed a fist
against one of the consoles. "I turned you back on!" he
shouted over the din. "What more do you want?!"

He turned but Kellen was already dashing up the stairs.
He followed her and moments later they burst out the door
of the force-field tower. They had barely gotten clear of it
when half a dozen of the Emperor's guards showed up,
shoved in a pass card, and entered the tower.

Gambler whistled in relief, and then realized that the
alarm was now sounding throughout the city, and that all
around him people were running about as if they were
headless chickens.

He turned to Kellen and grabbed her by the shoulders.
"What's happened? What's going on?"

"Don't talk to me like that," she snapped. He was
taken aback by her tone. "You don't have the right," she
said. "You're just a soldier. You're titleless."

His lips curling back in fury, he said, "And you'll be
toothless if you don't tell me what's happening."

"It's the city alarm," she said. "It means we're under
attack." Her voice trembled in fear. Whether it was because they were being attacked or because she was terri-
fied of what her father would do to her when he found out,
it was difficult to say.

"Attack! By whom?"

He turned his gaze skyward, and three dark shapes
appeared as pinspots in the heavens and started to grow
larger.

"Arrians!" he whispered hoarsely.

Bhodi and Leon stopped dead in their tracks, the sound
of alarms from the city reaching them even at their distance.

They looked at each other. "I don't like the sound of
that," said Bhodi. "Let's head back."

This time they did not run lightly but took the distance
in great ground-covering leaps, powered by the strength in

their Photon-energized legs. When they'd covered half the distance, there was a sudden warning scream of air overhead.

They looked up. Five hundred feet above them, flying towards the city at full speed, were three Dark Destroyers. They were flying single file, powerdiving towards the city.

"Holy crow!" shouted Bhodi. "Leon, we're in deep trouble!"

"Not as deep as they are," said Leon evenly. As he spoke he raised his bazooka upward, calmly making adjustments to range and intensity. "You know, Bhodi, there are a lot more Arrians than there are us. But the big thing about them that you can always count on . . ."

The ships were almost upon them and in a split instant would be past them. And yet, as if he had all the time in the world, Leon raised and activated his phaser bazooka.

A beam of pure Photon energy cut straight upward, directly in the path of the Dark Destroyers.

They tried to swerve out of the way but it was far too late. One after another they cut across the unmoving beam and Leon's phaser bazooka precisely sheered off their stabilizers.

The upshot of this was that the Dark Destroyers veered wildly out of control and began a swift plummet downward.

". . . is their incredible stupidity," finished Leon, as he shut off the bazooka.

The three ships spiraled downward and, with a resounding crash, landed behind a small group of mountains. Dark black smoke billowed forth, and Leon let out a full-throated cheer.

"Come on, Bhodi!" bellowed Leon. "Let's go finish them off." With overwhelming enthusiasm he charged in the direction of where the ships had crashed.

"Leon, wait!" shouted Bhodi.

"What for?" said Leon. "They've had the fight knocked out of them. Now all that's left is the mopping—"

With a howl of fury, over a hundred Soldarrs poured

over the hills, firing phaser blasts. Behind them, using their superior strength to haul actual cannons from the Dark Destroyer's armaments, came the Dark Guardians in full strength.

"—up?" finished Leon weakly.

The great Lizoid spun and headed as fast as he could for the city. Bhodi laid down a field of phaser fire to cover him, but he was too far away to hit anything accurately. The plus side of this was that the Warlord's forces were also too distant to hit them or the city.

Bhodi and Leon ran as fast as they could. The great doors of the city loomed before them . . . and they were swinging shut.

Bhodi got there first just as the doors were almost shut. He placed himself in front of the swinging doors and pitted his Photon strength against the massive power of the door, to slow it so that Leon could make it in to the safety of the city.

It was no contest. Bhodi might as well have been trying to take out a battle cruiser with spitballs. "Leon!" he shouted. "I can't hold it!"

Suddenly the door stopped, halted by a glow of energy.

Directly behind Bhodi, holding the door open with the power of his staff, Baethan stood concentrating against the irresistible push of hidden wheels and levers.

Leon shoved his way in and grabbed Bhodi in the crook of one huge arm. Baethan released his magical hold, and the door slammed shut with a resounding clang.

Leon dropped Bhodi to the ground. "Nice effort, Bhodi. Thanks for the assist, Baethan."

Baethan inclined his head slightly in acknowledgment. "It appears we are under siege."

Bhodi smacked a fist against the door. It was made from the same gleaming metal that constituted the rest of the protective wall. "Seems sturdy," he observed.

"Did you seriously expect to be able to knock it over with your fist, Bhodi Li?" asked Baethan.

"Uh . . . no. I guess not." He looked up the wall's great height. "What's this thing made out of?"

"Duranium," said Baethan.

"Is it tough?"

"When it was constructed several hundred years ago, there was no weapon capable of putting a hole in it."

"And now?"

"Now . . ." Baethan paused. "It would be advisable to develop a backup plan. Quickly."

13

The Light
Breaks

"It's your fault, Warriarr," snarled Mandarr. "How could you have been so stupid?"

Warriarr waved him off impatiently, studying the wall from a distance. "A minor setback."

"Minor setback! Our ships were destroyed, all because you were so intent on powerdiving to this planet, with all energy to speed, that you forgot to instruct everyone to raise their shields! So we get blown out of the sky by one Photon Guardian! I would call that more than a small setback, wouldn't you?"

"Not when we capture the city, it won't be." He gestured. "How long do you think that wall can survive bombardment from our weapons? We salvaged the main phaser guns—that gives us six guns capable of blasting Class 12 starships into random scraps. Add to that the hand-held firepower of the 112 Soldarrs who survived the crash, and our own weapons. We can take over the capital in a matter of hours. Less. So stop your whining and marshal the Soldarrs. The longer we leave them be, the longer they'll have to mount some sort of defense.'' He scanned the area once more. ''Fortunately, with the doors closed, they've cut themselves off from the spaceport. If they could reach the various vehicles parked there, they might have a fighting chance. As it is, they have no chance at all.''

''What are our chances, Parcival?''

''Slim to none.''

They were seated dismally with the Emperor in Central Control, studying the monitors that were focused on the army massing outside of the city.

''That's a pretty depressing assessment, Parcival,'' observed Tivia. ''Before we make any such pronouncements, let's examine all the options.''

The Emperor, who had been stalking back and forth in irritation, turned and started ticking off points on his fingers. ''Very well, my dear. Option one: Hope that our wall holds them off indefinitely. Well, we aren't prepared for a lengthy siege, and besides their weaponry can lay waste to our precious wall. Option two: Take them on. Well, in case you haven't noticed, my personal guard numbers exactly twenty. Their weapons are nowhere in the class of the Soldarrs. There are perhaps eight hundred people in the city, but they do not have any armament. So unless you propose to arm my people with shovels and sticks to take on the Arrians, then that is not workable either. Option three: Surrender. I'm not wild about that either.'' He paused and shook his head. ''What I still want to know is how they managed to sabotage the force field. What happened that caused it to fail for those fatal seconds?''

Bhodi glanced over at Gambler, and to his deepest dismay saw Gambler refusing to meet his gaze. Bhodi closed his eyes in pain. Aw, no, he thought. Not again.

Gambler turned to him then, saw the expression in his eyes, and then put that secretive finger to his lips.

Bhodi got to his feet, but before he could say anything,

Leon asked, "What about the other cities? Can we expect any help from them?"

The Emperor snorted. "The nearest city is 200 miles away. They're no better equipped for war than we are, and besides they're busy shoring up their own meager defenses." He leaned forward, his elbows on the table. "You realize that if they capture this city, they'll demolish the one force-field generator here and put a permanent hole in our planetary defenses. Once that happens, the Warlord will come in here with hundreds of ships and sweep over this planet like a black wave. And where will your precious Photon Alliance be then?" He stabbed a finger at Baethan. "You have to get me out of this. You owe it to me."

"Look," said Gambler, getting to his feet, "why don't we just go out there and take them on. So what if they outnumber us twelve to one? Let's try and pick them off while they're still outside."

They looked at each other. "It's a possibility," admitted Pike. "There are parapets along the top of the wall. We can go there and fire down on them. I'm sure that it will take them some time before they decide on a course of action, and—"

Suddenly one of the monitors flashed with light so blinding that it filled the room. Sirens began to sound throughout the city, and the city controller ran up to the Emperor, his face ashen. "They've started firing on the wall, sir," he said.

"How's it holding up?"

"It's starting to buckle."

The Emperor threw up his arms. "Oh, that's just marvelous. Just fantastic."

Baethan said, command in his voice. "Evacuate your citizens from their homes. Regroup them and keep them all in your palace. It's heavily shielded, large enough, and the farthest point from the main gate where the attack is being concentrated. We shall be your first line of defense.

We will try to take out as many of them as possible before we fall, so as to leave as few as possible for your guards.''

"What did he mean, before we fall?" asked Gambler.

"Instruct your guards to aim at the power plates on the chests of the Soldarrs and Dark Guardians. They are projectons, and a direct hit on their power plates will disrupt the energy flow from Arr and send them back to the Warlord. Understood?"

"What if we hit them in the head or body?"

"That may or may not stop the Soldarrs, because they may or may not be real. It depends upon the whim of the Warlord. But the Dark Guardians most certainly are projectons, and the only way to stop them is hitting the power plates.''

The Emperor nodded. "All right." He paused. "I just want all of you to know—I know I'm difficult sometimes. Subject to whim. Impossible to predict, arrogant, even mercurial. But I just want you to know—you are the bravest souls it has been my honor to know."

Baethan nodded. "Thank you, Emperor. Let us all do what we have to."

Gambler tapped Bhodi on the shoulder. "What did he mean by 'When we fall'?"

Bhodi pulled away from him. "Don't you talk to me."

"But—"

"I don't want to hear it." He turned on his heel and left Gambler standing there by himself.

The buildings were deserted, all the people having been ushered into the palace. Gambler walked alone, looking around, thinking about the last time he had seen Kellen—ushering the aged and crippled in through the palace doors. She had been all business then, and there had been something about her—a certain, indefinable something that told him beyond any doubt that he was not in her league.

The Photon Warriors had scattered themselves throughout the city. They were hoping that picking off the Soldarrs from hiding would be an effective way to whittle down their numbers. The drawback was that it meant splitting up their strength, but they couldn't have it both ways.

Gambler stopped in the main square and looked up dismally at the giant Photon prism gleaming in the light. In the distance he heard the pounding of the cannons against the main doors. They weren't going to last much longer, he thought. He realized that he was the last Photon Warrior between the Arrians and the palace. The last line of defense.

He stared at his Photon phaser. "I didn't bargain for this," he said out loud.

"No," came a voice from behind him. "I bet you didn't."

He turned. "Hi, Bhodi."

Bhodi walked towards him slowly. "Hi, Bhodi? That's it? No smooth remarks? No cute rhymes? What's the matter? Staring at death through overwhelming odds getting you down?" He stepped up close to him. "Blast it, you lied to me!"

"No."

"Don't deny it! I don't know how or why yet, but it probably had something to do with Kellen. You've put us all in danger because you only cared about yourself. And you know what really steams me? It's my fault too, because I could have done something about you and I didn't."

"That's your problem, Bhodi."

"It's all our problem! That's our problem, knocking on our front door."

There was a heart-rending crunching of metal and Bhodi winced. "There's not much time left. You'd better pick a vantage point and get ready."

Anger and fury smoldered in Gambler's face. "It's not fair!" he blurted out. "Why should I die because of these good-for-nothings, hiding in the palace like scared rabbits?"

"Because that's our job," said Bhodi tersely.

"Well, it's not mine!" yelled Gambler. "I hate this planet and I hate that Kellen and I hate their stupid prism—I hate all of it." He spun, yanked out his phaser and fired point-blank at the towering prism.

The phaser beam hit it on one polished side, refracted and splintered out the other. A thousand beams of light shot off in a thousand different directions, slicing through buildings and leaving holes wherever they went. It was a dazzling array of color and power, and then it halted as abruptly as it started.

"Are you crazy?" demanded Bhodi, slapping the phaser down.

"I'm sorry," he said, but he didn't sound it.

"Look, watch what you're doing. You could have . . ."

His voice trailed off and he looked off into the distance in astonishment. "Of course," he whispered. And then he said louder, "Of course!"

He turned to Gambler, excitement bubbling through him. "Wait here! Don't move! Wait here."

He bolted down the main street of Dekka, shouting as loudly as he could. "Regroup! Regroup at the town square!"

In their individual hiding places, the Photon Warriors looked out in surprise. Bhodi was moving as quickly as he could, shouting, "I have an idea! Get down to the Photon prism! Hurry! There isn't much time."

Just ahead of him there was a sudden tearing of metal, a groan like the souls of a thousand people being ripped raw from their bodies, and then there were the sounds of shots being fired.

Baethan. Baethan was at the point, the first line of defense.

"Baethan!" he shouted. "Baethan, wherever you are, get down here!"

He scanned the buildings overhead, trying to determine where Baethan was firing from, and then suddenly phaser bolts shot past him.

Bhodi leaped to one side and hid inside the doorway of

one of the abandoned buildings. Soldarrs rounded the corner, and from hiding Bhodi started to pick them off. One, two, then four, and as he nailed each one, they would give a little screech, a half turn of their body and discorporate. They didn't break up into a thousand little swirls of color, like the Dark Guardians did. They just popped out of existence. Bhodi wondered for the umpteenth time just what the Soldarrs were, anyway.

"Aha!"

Before Bhodi could turn, he'd been grabbed from behind by four powerful arms. He clung frantically to his phaser even as his desperate mind told him that he had been snagged by Warriarr.

"Didn't expect me to come up behind you, did you, Bhodi Li?" snarled Warriarr in his ear.

Bhodi swung his phaser around, jammed it straight into Warriarr's mouth and fired.

The impact blew Warriarr back, forcing him to drop Bhodi. Pain shot through Bhodi's shoulder—Warriarr may have wrenched his right arm.

He stared at Warriarr with horrific fascination. The blast had ripped off the top of the projecton's head, but already it was beginning to reform. Red leathery skin reknit itself, a lost eye started to regenerate.

So that was what was meant by projectons being impossible to kill. They were self-repairing. Insanely, Bhodi wished he had a car that could do that.

They were inside a small room and Warriarr staggered to his feet. Bhodi, leaning against the door that led outside, tried to bring his arm up to aim and pain ripped through. Wrenched indeed—it might have been dislocated. Bhodi flipped his phaser to his left hand and fired, but his aim was nowhere near as good. He nailed Warriarr in his upper left arm and the phaser beam sliced it through. Even as it fell to the floor another one started to grow.

Warriarr lurched toward him, howling in pain and fury. Closing one eye, Bhodi fired. He hit Warriarr's chest plate directly, and the four-armed Dark Guardian, realizing his time was up, made one last desperate attempt to murder Bhodi. Even as his body started to dissolve, Warriarr leaped. Bhodi threw up his left arm to protect himself and suddenly was surrounded in a shower of sparks—the last remains of Warriarr as he went howling back to the Warlord in disgrace.

"Better you than me, pal," muttered Bhodi, as he hauled himself up and dashed out the door.

He ran and fired as Soldarrs congregated at the top of the street. Mandarr spotted him and yelled, "There he is!" just as a great bolt of energy cut across the space in front of them, driving them back. Baethan had come out of hiding and now cut an imposing figure as he stood next to Bhodi, blasting left and right with his staff. "I hope," he said curtly, "that you have some major reason for totally violating the plan we had so carefully worked out."

"Would survival be a good enough reason?" asked Bhodi, firing off random shots with his phaser in his left hand.

"Sufficient."

"All right. We have to lead them to the town square, where the Photon prism is. It's our best chance."

They started to run, dodging back and forth and covering for each other as the Soldarrs bore down on them in hot pursuit. Several shots ricocheted off of Bhodi's armor, but if they managed to get a clean hit at an exposed area, that would be all for him.

Baethan turned once, stopped and slammed his staff down with all his might on the ground. Tremors issued forth and shook the street violently, knocking the Soldarrs and the Dark Guardians off their feet. During that time Baethan and Bhodi managed to gain some distance on their pursuers.

"Bhodi!" Tivia shouted from nowhere. "Where are you going?"

"Got another plan. Fall back," he gasped out.

Tivia appeared, unwrapping her cloak of invisibility from around herself. Bhodi shook his head. "I wish you'd had that thing when we were in Nazi Germany. It would have made life a lot easier."*

She fell in behind them, and the street seemed to shake with the pursuing hordes of Arrians. "This plan," gasped Tivia, "who came up with it?"

"I did," said Bhodi.

He heard a moan from her that indicated her confidence in him had crept back down to acceptable levels.

As they ran, they picked up Pike, Parcival and Leon as each of them came out of their respective hiding places and joined the headlong rush of the Photon Guardians down the street. "I told you that you always had to keep your retreat in practice," Leon said to Bhodi. Bhodi merely nodded a brief acknowledgment.

They circled the arena, and Tivia shouted, "Baethan! Can you cast an illusion to disguise the pit so that the Arrians won't see it and fall into it?"

"For something of this size? Not enough time," said Baethan.

"Don't worry," said Bhodi. "If this works, then we won't have any problems."

"And if it doesn't?" asked Parcival, hard on Bhodi's heels.

Bhodi shrugged. "Then we're no worse off than we were before."

They got to the town square and there the Photon prism loomed before them. "All right," said Bhodi, "here's the plan. Love it or leave it."

He explained quickly and, to his surprise (and to theirs, somewhat) the Photon Guardians acknowledged that it was indeed workable. Sometime during the quick briefing Gambler had shown up and taken his place with the Photon Guardians. Bhodi said nothing to him, and Gambler made

---

*See Book One, FOR THE GLORY

a display of saying nothing to Bhodi. The other Warriors, pressed as they were for time, didn't notice.

They all lined up on one side of the prism—the side away from where the Arrian warriors would be showing up. Their yelling and war whoops were audible as they drew closer and closer. Parcival was busy making calculations on his portable computer, and finally he pulled out his bat and said, "There. The ideal point to aim for is precisely thirty feet down and five feet inward." The end of his special bat flipped open to reveal a narrow phaser muzzle.

"Ready?" asked Bhodi. "Are we on Parcival's mark?"

They all acknowledged their readiness.

"Okay." Bhodi grinned. "Don't fire until you see the whites of Mandarr's eyes."

Leon chortled softly. "You can see the whites of Mandarr's eyes clear into the next galaxy."

The yelling drew closer, closer still.

"Steady," said Bhodi. "Wait until they're all together. Steady now."

"Bhodi?"

"Yes, Tivia?"

"Shut up."

"Yes, Tivia."

They came around the corner at the far end of the street then, the Soldarrs of the Warlord of Arr. There were still at least a hundred of them, and they all looked dressed to kill. Mixed in with them were the Dark Guardians, gloating in evil triumph at seeing their helpless enemies lined up like polite cattle waiting for the slaughter.

"Now!" said Bhodi.

They all fired precisely on the point that Parcival had instructed. Their beams joined as one, hit the target, refracted and came out the other side. It was a shocking, unnatural rainbow that shot out of the prism and enveloped the attacking Soldarrs.

"Keep pouring it on!" shouted Bhodi.

At first the sheer power of the light was enough to stagger the Arrians. They gasped from the brightness, felt the purity of the light peel away their sickened skin and cleanse their souls. Then came the rays. The thousands upon thousands of multicolored beams that sliced everywhere, hitting chest plates and power plates right and left and sending them one by one back to Arr. It was as if a horde of flying carpet tacks had been set loose in a balloon convention. They shrieked their indignations, their pain, their mortification, but none of it mattered. The air was alive with the glorious hum of the phaser beams doing their cleansing business.

The Soldarrs and the Dark Guardians had no defense at all. They batted at it as if it were a swarm of mosquitoes. None of it was to any avail, because within thirty seconds the last of the Arrians had vanished.

"Cease fire!" shouted Leon, and they did.

They surveyed the streets with great pleasure. "Parcival, take a sensor reading," suggested Pike.

Parcival touched a button on his wrist console that caused an antenna to project from his computer backpack. He studied his wrist monitor carefully before responding, "Clean. No Arrians."

"Who you gonna call?" crowed Bhodi. "Arr-Busters!"

"I'm glad you're enthusiastic, Bhodi," said Tivia. "But may I point out that we've lost something else as well, and I'm afraid that you're going to have to be the one who explains it to the Emperor."

"What are you talking a—oh."

They looked up at Emperor Flynn's most prized possession.

The prism, because of the intensity of the light being filtered through it, had developed a huge crack down its middle. It ran the length of the great prism. Furthermore, the exterior was now blackened and smoky. In short, it was no longer the thing of beauty of which the Emperor had been so proud.

"He said we should do whatever we had to do," said Bhodi. "How can he be mad at us when we follow instructions? After all," he said pointedly at Gambler, "we know what happens when we don't."

14

Et Tu, Bhodi?

They could barely push their way into the palace, there were so many people. But push they did, spreading the news as they went that all was safe, that the Arrians had been safely dispatched back to their home planet. As a result there was a ground swell of cheering that accompanied them as they approached the throne room, where the Emperor at that moment was holding court.

They were there, the Emperor and all his daughters, and he looked up anxiously as they entered. "Well?" he asked, trying to mask his nervousness. "Are they right behind you? What has happened? Where do we stand?"

"On extremely solid ground, Majesty," said Baethan. "They're gone."

An explosive cheer went up from around the room. Before it could get too out of hand, Baethan put up one large hand, gesturing for silence. "We did, however," he intoned, "have one casualty. Your prism."

The Emperor seemed staggered, as if hit with a hammer. "My . . . prism?" he asked, and slowly seated himself. "Tell me what happened. Everything."

Leon stepped forward, since Leon was generally regarded as the best storyteller in the group. In quick, broad strokes he described the battle that they'd just had, and when he got to the part about the prism being cracked and blackened, the Emperor looked as if he were about to have a stroke.

He leaped to his feet, tears welling in his eyes. His voice rose as he shouted, "Make no mistake, my people! My gratitude to these brave souls knows no bounds. The sacrifice of my gem," his voice choked, and he looked at his daughters, all lined up nearby, "is a minor one to make compared to the safety of you, my subjects. But I demand to know who it is who has brought us to this point. Who caused the shield to fall? Who must take responsibility for that action?"

No one spoke. It was possible that no one even breathed.

Bhodi turned to Gambler and waited for him to say something. Gambler stared at him, wide-eyed and innocent-looking, and gave him a slow, broad wink. Then he folded his arms and looked around, as if expecting the guilty party to step out of the crowd somewhere and admit to his duplicity.

And Bhodi stepped forward and said, "I know who was responsible." He turned and pointed. "It was Gambler."

There was a gasp from the crowd and protests of shock from the Photon Guardians. They all spoke at once, the foremost being Tivia who said, "Bhodi, have you lost your mind?"

But he ignored them all. They might as well have not been there. It was just Bhodi and Gambler, staring at each other, and Gambler slowly shaking his head, a look of total disappointment on his face.

"I thought you were my friend," Gambler said in a low, angry voice. "How can you accuse me of this?"

"Because it's true," was the taut reply.

"You have no proof," Gambler said, and then louder, to the entire crowd, he said, "He has no proof of this! It's a lie. In fact, I say Bhodi Li was responsible. Yeah. Somehow he caused the force field to fail, and he's afraid he'll be found out. So he's trying to shift blame to me."

Leon said, "But that's ridiculous, he was with me when the shield broke down," but no one heard him. The entire palace had filled with the swell of babbling voices, and the Emperor was shouting at the top of his lungs. Bhodi couldn't quite make out what he was saying, but he could take a pretty good guess.

They faced each other in the area.

They had left their weapons at the top, with their fellow Warriors. Parcival had been saying, "Neither of you has to do this."

"Yes, we do," said Bhodi. "Aside from the fact that it's planetary law—it's something that we both have to do."

Gambler had said nothing, but merely glared at Bhodi, anger filling his scarlet eyes.

They faced each other now, down in the pit. Now, where no one could easily hear them, Gambler stood several yards from Bhodi and said, with hurt in his voice, "How could you have done it? We could have both walked away from this, man."

"Because what you did was wrong," said Bhodi. "And you endangered yourself, and you endangered others. You had to be stopped, here and now."

"You won't be able to," said Gambler. "I'll win, and then they'll throw you out of the Guardians and I'll be rid of you. And I won't miss you at all, because I thought you were my friend and you crossed me up. Friends don't rat."

They circled each other cautiously. "If being a rat means being concerned about the safety of others, then yeah. I guess I am a rat," said Bhodi. "But better that than a dead rat."

"No. You're a dead duck."

Gambler hardly seemed to move, and suddenly he had covered the distance between himself and Bhodi. Bhodi swung wide, missed completely and Gambler smacked him hard on the side of the head. Stars exploded in front of him and he went down on his knees, gasping. Nearby he saw Gambler standing there, laughing, and there was a roaring in his head. Maybe it was the crowd and maybe it was the blood to his brain. He ignored it and swung out with one leg, trying to knock Gambler to his back.

Gambler leaped lightly over the leg sweep and Bhodi scrambled to his feet. Gambler swung and Bhodi ducked, only to realize too late that Gambler was feinting and his real blow was coming now, a fierce front snapkick that caught Bhodi in the pit of his stomach and knocked the air out of him. He staggered and Gambler rabbit-punched him on the back of the neck.

He groaned, his vision blurring and darkness reaching out for him. He pushed it away and tried to get to his feet and another punch to the point of his jaw rattled his head. He felt blood welling in his mouth and reached out, desperately and blindly.

He lucked out, catching Gambler's right arm just as Gambler was about to give another brutal shot to Bhodi's head. He grabbed it as if it were a life preserver, and with a yell he pulled Gambler towards him while slamming a knee upward. It caught Gambler in the gut, and Bhodi heard a satisfying "Whoompf" as he knocked Gambler's breath out. He held on desperately with his left hand and kneed Gambler again. His right arm still ached from his fight with Warriarr, but Bhodi used it now and hit Gambler in the face as hard as he could.

Gambler went down, but Bhodi lost his grip on Gambler's arm and the blue-skinned Photon Guardian rolled away. He bounced to his feet, but now they faced each

other battered, lungs fighting raggedly for air. Bhodi's
vision had cleared, and he wished he was wearing his
helmet, but that had been removed along with his gun
when they'd been sent down into the pit.

"Give up, Gambler," he spit out. "It's over."

"That's right!" howled Gambler. "Over for you!"

He leaped toward Bhodi and started to turn in midair.
Bhodi realized that he was trying that same reverse kick
he'd seen him use on Baethan. It was a devastating blow if
delivered, but the disadvantage was that in your spin you
had to take your eyes off your opponent for just a moment.
In that moment Bhodi got out of the way, so when Gambler followed through, his foot contacted only empty air.
He landed off balance, and Bhodi stepped in and slammed
his left fist as hard as he could into Gambler's solar plexus.
Gambler staggered and Bhodi hit him again, as hard as he
could, so hard he thought his fist would break.

Gambler fell back and Bhodi leaped around him, wrapping his arms around Gambler's neck and shoulders and
bringing him to the ground. Within seconds he had Gambler pinned. Gambler writhed in his grip but it didn't do
any good. Bhodi didn't let up the pressure in the least.

"Admit it," grated Bhodi. "Admit it or I'll break your
neck."

"No, you won't!" said Gambler. "First off, you're not
holding me right, and second, you wouldn't anyway." He
struggled in Bhodi's lock, arching his back, trying to
obtain some sort of leverage and failing. He yelled as
loudly as he could. "This doesn't prove anything! So he
can beat up on me. Big deal! I'm still innocent as far as
I'm concerned!"

The Emperor looked down on them, and then there was
a feather touch on his arm. He turned and Kellen was
looking at him, her face set, and she was shaking her
head.

"Father," she said softly, "I have a confession to
make."

He raised an eyebrow. "Oh?"

"Yes. I was seeing Gambler behind your back, because you're always so possessive of us it just makes me sick. And I stole your pass key into the force-field generator so that Gambler and I could have some privacy, because he wanted to . . . well, you know. And anyway, there was so much noise and Gambler wanted everything to be just right for me, and besides, all the racket was making him crazy, so he shut down all the force-field generators, and that's how the hole appeared and the Arrians managed to attack and almost destroyed us and the Photon Guardians and the entire Alliance, and almost brought darkness to the entire universe forever."

He stared at her, long and hard. He looked back down into the pit. Gambler had seen her talking to him and had stopped struggling, clearly waiting for the result of what she had been saying to him. Bhodi was watching too, but he wasn't letting up the pressure on his hold.

The Emperor looked around him. At the people who had almost been slaughtered. At the buildings which had been devastated. At his beautiful prism, created to celebrate Kellen's birth, now cracked and ruined.

He looked back at her and, weighing each word carefully, said, "You are grounded for the rest of your life."

15
Deceptions

Gambler turned with preternatural speed and fired on his enemy. The phaser blast knocked his opponent's gear out of commission, and Gambler darted away, still not having been nailed by enemy fire.

Bhodi watched him with a great heaviness in his heart. They were back in Intellistar, watching Gambler back in his Photon Center at Kenilwurth. Yet Bhodi couldn't help but remember the conversation they'd had when they'd been pulled out of the pit, surrounded by the other Photon Warriors.

"I thought I could trust you," Gambler had told him. "Maybe I did make mistakes. Maybe my judgment was bad. But I thought you were supposed to help me until I got some real experience under my belt. I thought I could count on you to cover for me. Instead you crossed me up."

"It was for your own good."

"My own good! What a laugh. Look, I made up for it, didn't I? I was the one who gave you the idea to use the

Photon prism—an idea I didn't hear you giving me any credit for, by the way. Maybe I've gotten us into messes, but I've always cleaned up after them. I even saved your life, and Tivia's. You owe me, and this is how you repay your debts. Well, thanks a lot. Some friend you turned out to be.''

The words echoed in his mind now as he watched Gambler many light-years away. ''MOM?'' he asked softly.

''Yes, Bhodi Li?'' Her voice came from all around him.

''Are you sure he won't remember a thing?''

''Absolutely. I wiped from his mind all his experiences as a Photon Guardian. After all, if one has found the Light only to lose it, it seems a rather cruel memory to have to carry along.''

''Yeah. I guess.''

He was quiet for a time, watching the carefree Gambler, and thought about when his own life had been that simple. Just the game of Photon, that was all. There was nothing confusing then, no inner turmoil to turn his stomach into knots. Just Red team versus Green team, and may the more accurate phaser win.

He didn't hear Tivia come up behind him, but only heard her soft voice say, ''Bhodi Li?''

''Ah, look, Tivia . . . I'm not in the mood right now. Okay?''

She stood next to him and watched Gambler on the screen. ''You really liked him, didn't you?''

''I thought he was my friend,'' said Bhodi. ''He thought I was his. There's one great rule, and that's that friends don't turn against each other. I crossed him up and he felt betrayed.''

''He betrayed you as well.''

''That doesn't make me feel any better.''

''I didn't think it would.'' She paused. ''Your loyalty is admirable, Bhodi. It's what makes you such a good warrior. It's also what makes you a liability sometimes, because you'll risk your life in order to save one of your friends. But that's part of you. Sometimes, though, you have to weigh your responsibility to a friend against the best interests of all concerned, including that friend. You have to do what you know is right, no matter how difficult that might be for you."

He looked up at her. "Covering for Gambler—even when I was doing it, it never felt right to me."

"There you are," she said. "If you know in your heart that something is wrong, then all the excuses you make for it in your head aren't going to make it right."

He nodded. "I guess so." He patted her hand. "Thanks, Tivia." And then, as he stood, he said, "Are you going to miss him?"

"Oh, definitely. If for no other reason, I'm going to miss all the awful lines he kept giving you that were supposed to work on me."

She turned and left Bhodi with his mouth hanging open.

After a few moments Bhodi began to laugh. Then, still laughing, he walked out into the hallways of Intellistar.

"Pike!" he called out. "Parcival! Tivia!"

He heard MOM's voice. "They've all left, Bhodi. And now it's time for you to return home, too."

Seeing his opportunity, Bhodi said, "MOM. There have been a lot of things I've been thinking about lately. A lot of things I wanted to ask you about, but haven't really had the chance."

"Things, Bhodi?"

"Yeah. Like for instance, how come the Warlord never tries to attack us directly? I mean, if I were him, that's what I would do."

"Then I suppose we must be grateful that you are not he," said MOM reasonably. "It's time for you to go back, Bhodi."

"But I had a question about the time-freezing, too. And—"

"The Light shines, Bhodi."

Before he could say another word, Bhodi's molecules

turned and twisted back on themselves, and within an instant he was gone. Intellistar sat empty once again.

Christopher Jarvis sat at home that evening reading a book, an unusual pastime for Chris, but he decided to give it a shot. He'd heard the book was pretty good.

As he did, he thought about the end of his mission and suddenly realized that he'd been in the middle of a conversation with MOM when he'd left. He closed the book, which was titled *Knight Life*, and pondered a moment, trying to remember what it was he had been talking about. But he couldn't. How very odd, because he had the vague, uncomfortable feeling that it had been something pretty important.

There was a loud honk outside, and Chris ignored it until he heard Al's voice shouting out to him. "Hey, Jarvis! Get out here! Right now!" This was followed by another insistent honk. "The moon is full and the night is young. Let's move!"

Chris tossed the book aside and ran out the front door. There was Al hanging out the window of his dad's Porsche. He had a wide grin on his face. "Chris! My main man. Hop in and let's go for a whirl."

Christopher stuck his head in and looked around the interior of the car. There were several beer cans lying on the seat next to Al.

"How many beers have you had, Al?" he demanded.

Al stared at the empties next to him as if seeing them for the first time. "It's not me!" he said. "Honest. It's the car."

"The car?"

"Yeah. The car. It runs on Miller Lite. Honest."

Chris nodded, unimpressed. "Get out of the car, Al."

Al stared at him as if he'd just grown a second nose. "What do you mean, get out of the car? It's my car."

"No. It's your father's car. It is, however, your life, and I'm going to make sure that you hold on to it."

He reached in and pulled the keys from the ignition.

"Hey!" howled Al, and he fumbled for the door latch and leaped out of the car. "What the do do you think you're hecking?"

"What I'm 'hecking'," said Chris, "is making sure you get home in one piece. I'm calling you a cab."

Outraged, Al followed Chris into the house. "A cab! You can't call me a cab. Cabs aren't cool!"

"Neither are hospital emergency wards," said Chris as he entered the house, Al staggering in after him. "Or morgues, or cemeteries. Which is where you'll wind up unless I do something about it."

As he picked up the phone and started to dial, Al plopped down on a couch nearby. "Aw, man, I thought you were my friend."

"Hey, don't try to make me feel guilty," said Chris. "I've had experts try that." He turned back to the phone. "Hi, cab service? I'd like you to send a taxi to . . ."

He heard deep snoring behind him. He turned and saw that Al had passed out on the couch.

Now here was an interesting problem. Chris could get Al taxied home, get his car towed or even drive it himself—it wasn't far. He knew that by the following morning Al's parents would be back home from visiting their out-of-town friends, because Al had told him so.

Chris shrugged and said to the taxi service. "Forget it. Thanks anyway. Bye."

He hung up, picked Al up, slung him over his shoulder and brought him upstairs to his bedroom. He tossed him on the extra bed, and Al bounced like a sack of potatoes and lay still. His snoring continued loudly.

Chris was thankful that his folks and sister had gone out to a movie. It would have been a real panic trying to handle all this with them home to further complicate matters. When they arrived, well, Al staying over was nothing new. Everything would be cool until morning. Chris went back downstairs to pick up his book and continue reading.

• • •

Chris was awakened the next morning by a low moan. He rolled over, and Al was sitting up in the next bed, rubbing his skull and groaning to himself, "Aw, man, did you get the license of that truck that ran over my head?"

"Morning, Al," said Chris, sitting up.

"Yeah, yeah. Yeeech. My mouth feels like I gargled with toxic waste. Hey—I owe you for this one. I didn't realize how blotto I'd gotten. If you hadn't pulled me out of the car—"

"I know. They would have pulled you out of a wreck."

Chris's phone rang, and Al fell back, the ringing of the phone cutting straight through his head. Chris grabbed up the phone.

"Jarvis residence and drunk tank," he said, casting a glance at his hung-over friend. "How can I help you?"

"Chris," came the worried voice of Al's mother. "We just got back from visiting my folks, and Al isn't here. Is he there by any chance?"

He glanced over and mouthed the words, "It's your mom." Al groaned louder. "Yes, he's here, Mrs. Fedder. No problem on that."

He heard Al's mother say with relief, "He's there," doubtlessly to Al's dad. Then Mr. Fedder came on the line and he didn't sound quite as sympathetic. "Chris, is my car there, too, by any chance?"

"Hold on, Mr. Fedder." Placing his hand over the receiver, he said, "Your father wants to know about his car."

Al covered his eyes. "Stall him, Chris. Say something. Anything. I'll go ditch the car, and I can tell him it was stolen again. Or—"

But Chris was shaking his head. "It's your responsibility, man. I'm not covering for you on this."

"Hey, you're supposed to be my friend," said Al.

"I am. I was enough of a friend to make sure you didn't wind up in a body bag. The rest is up to you."

Al scowled at him darkly, and then his face softened. "I guess you're right. I just have to face up to it. Take it like a man."

He took the phone and said, "Hello?" Then he paused. "They tell me you're my father. I'm afraid I . . . I have amnesia. Everything is a blank to me."

Chris moaned and fell back in his bed. Some guys, he reasoned, would just never learn.

Far off on Intellistar the corridors now sat empty. The soft lights of MOM's computer face blinked on and off on the main console.

Then a soft laugh filled Intellistar. A soft, evil laugh that grew louder and louder. The lights on MOM's board flashed frantically and then abruptly went from soft blue and red and yellow to deepest black.

The laugh became all-consuming, triumphant, and then stopped.

The lights from MOM's board had vanished. All of Intellistar went dead at the same time.

Her rotation halted, and slowly Intellistar began to drift, dead in space.

MOM was gone. And the mocking laughter echoed through Intellistar.

Next

With MOM gone, can the rest of the Photon Alliance be far behind? Learn the true origins of Photon! Learn who programmed MOM! Follow Bhodi Li and the Photon Warriors as they desperately go where no Photon Warrior has gone before:

IN SEARCH OF MOM